STUPEFYING STORIES 25

A RAMPANT LOON PRESS PUBLICATION

Editor in Chief: Bruce Bethke

Guiding Light: Karen Bethke

Editorial Assistant: Sharon Cherri

Consigliere: Henry Vogel

Motivational Coach: Pete Wood

Social Media Director: Eric Dontigney

Special Thanks to: The Fearless Slush Pile Reader Corps. They also serve who read and reject the dreck. *Thank you!*

Extra Special Thanks to: Brandon Nolta, for help and support above and beyond the call of friendship.

Cover art: ©grandfailure/Adobe Stock

September 2023: Vol. 1, No. 25

STUPEFYING STORIES is a production of RAMPANT LOON PRESS and is published in the United States of America by Rampant Loon Press, an imprint of Rampant Loon Media LLC, P.O. Box 111, Lake Elmo, Minnesota 55042.

www.rampantloonmedia.com

ISBN:
978-1-958333-12-9 ebook
978-1-958333-13-6 print

Contents

A few words from the editor...

Wow, another new issue *already?* It seems like just last month we were looking at *Stupefying Stories 24* sitting there on the launch pad, fully fueled and ready to go, and wondering whether it was going to soar like an eagle or blow up in our faces when we pushed the big red button.

Now, here we are again, counting down the minutes to the launch of *Stupefying Stories 25* and feeling much more confident this time. The magazine itself continues to evolve, with scads of little technical improvements under the skin that you can't readily see but that make it much better and easier for us to build. Our new editorial team is really coming together and starting to hit their stride. Submissions are continuing to stream in for issues 26, 27, and 28, and we're actually managing to handle the submissions pipeline *and* publish new fiction at the same time, which is a thing we have never been able to do smoothly before.

If you've been following our blog (stupefyingstories.blogspot.com) or me personally on Facebook, you have some idea of how hard it has been for us to get this point. If you haven't been following our blog, you should be, if only to catch **SHOWCASE**, our daily free flash fiction feature. We're publishing a lot of great little stories in *SHOWCASE* and growing a really good community around it, and if you like short fiction, you owe it to yourself to check out the stories and join the conversation. *SHOWCASE* is also turning out to be a great place for us to find and recruit the writers we want to feature in the pages of our magazine—

And speaking of magazines, I need to tell you how excited I am about **STUPEFYING STORIES 25.** We have a great mix of stories in this issue, by a great mix of returning fan-favorite authors and writers who are new to our pages.

If you're looking for science fiction that's so hard it clanks, check out **"A Limited View"** by **Gary Kloster** or **"Something Came Through"** by **Michael D. Burnside**. If you're looking for something that's still hard SF but with more of a biological angle, read **"There Is Another Sky"** by **Bo Balder**. If your tastes run to steampunk, read **"Cloudbreaker Above"** by **Brandon Nolta**, or if you like to relax with a tall glass of cold horror, read **"The Demolition Job"** by **Neva Bryan**.

If you like fantasy, check out **"Two-Tone"** by **Elise Stephens**. In this story Elise introduces us to a new form of magic *and* tells a beautiful and heart-breaking story, which is something we don't see often. If you're a bit more jaded about romance, read **"The Wawa Stick"** by **Karl El-Koura**, a futuristic tale of crime, betrayal, and just desserts. If you want a foretaste of the kinds of stories we're selecting for issue #27, be sure to read **"Tin Lizzi"** by **J. L. Royce** and **"Caliban's Cameras"** by **Allan Dyen-Shapiro**.

But we decided to lead off this issue with fan-favorite author **Fred Coppersmith** and his contemporary fantasy story of two brothers who just can't seem to stop getting into magical trouble, **"If We Shadows."**

Enjoy!

Per aspera ad astra,

Bruce Bethke

If We Shadows

By Fred Coppersmith

"THE VEIL BETWEEN WORLDS HAS BEEN PARTED. YOU MIGHT WANT TO RUN."

Louis is sitting at the bar when he gets the note from his kid brother. It's folded twice, scribbled on a torn scrap of lined notebook paper, like they're in the goddamn tenth grade or something.

Manny hands him the paper with his plate of eggs and the beer that Louis needs to hide the taste of Manny's cooking, bottle of Tabasco at the side for when the beer inevitably fails. The bartender just looks at him and says, "I dunno, some guy was in earlier, asked me to hand this to you," then walks away with a shrug that says he isn't Louis' damn delivery service.

Louis recognizes Jake's crooked handwriting right away. How long's it been this time? Eight months? Maybe almost a year since he's seen his brother, since the last time Jake brought trouble back with him to town.

Louis pokes at his eggs, but he's lost his appetite for the soggy mess Manny tries to pass off as scrambled.

"This guy," Louis says, waving Manny over from the end of the bar, "he say anything else? Leave an address, a number?"

"I look like a friggin' message board?" Manny asks. "All he said was, he knew you'd be in later, said give that to you. That was, I dunno, around nine or ten this morning."

Louis nods, downs half the beer. He could hope Jake is just screwing with him, stopping by his usual haunts to throw a little scare into his older brother. It wouldn't be the first time.

But the Veil is a hell of a thing to joke about. If it really *is*

1

parted—really is *gone*—then running isn't going to do anybody the least bit of any good.

"Tell you this, though," Manny says, "guy kinda looked a little familiar. Like maybe I'd seen him someplace before?"

"Uh, yeah," Louis says, "that's kinda the definition of familiar."

"Nah, you know what I mean," Manny says. If he cares that Louis hasn't touched his food, he doesn't show it. "This guy, you know him?"

"Guy's my brother," Louis says, "so yeah, unfortunately I know him."

He throws back the rest of his glass, then pulls a twenty from his pocket and tosses that on the bar.

"You probably know him too," he says. "The name Jake Palmer mean anything?"

The bartender shakes his head. "Nah, I don't think so. Why? Who's that supposed to—"

And yeah, there it is, Louis thinks. That sudden shock of recognition. He can read it all over the bartender's face. Bad eggs or not, he's going to miss this bar.

"Oh hell," Manny says. "You're Louis *Palmer*?" He looks about half ready to punch Louis in the face. "You're those goddamn kids who broke into the Faerie kingdom all those years ago!"

"Yeah," Louis says. "That would be us."

Except they hadn't really broken, so much as stumbled, into that other world, a dumb accident right from the start.

Louis had been, what? Eleven? Already too old to really believe in faeries anymore, or at least in the stories about them their grandmother used to tell. He knew there'd been sightings, of course, in the dark thicket of woods behind the house. And he knew about the Faerie War, obviously. Everybody did. But *that* had been over a hundred years earlier. Everything since then was just ghost stories.

Jake was running ahead of Louis in the woods that morning, where what passed for a path narrowed and curved. They were a good mile or two from the highway, and far enough from the house that Louis couldn't see its yellow frame. Probably not even on their grandfather's property anymore, he thought when he finally caught up with Jake. More likely they'd strayed into the tight knot of trees between home and their nearest neighbor, that part of the woods that for a hundred years had gone unclaimed.

Old growth. Scorched earth.

Louis wasn't sure if he was remembering something he'd learned in school or in one of their grandmother's stories. Either way, the trees here were taller, the shadows deeper and darker, and a chill hung over everything like a cold hand pressing down on the back of your neck.

"What the hell are you doing?" Louis asked his brother.

"I'm gonna tell Poppy you cursed," Jake said. But he didn't turn around, or even glance at Louis when he said it, and instead just kept staring at something at the base of one of the bigger trees.

"Is it just me," Jake finally asked, "or does that thing look kinda like a door?"

He pointed near the tree's massive roots, each one thicker around than a fist. Sure enough, cut into the old growth of the trunk, maybe five feet tall and only half that wide, was a small rectangular shape that, if you looked at it a little sideways, might have resembled *something* like a door.

It was only the golden light that seemed to leak around the edges that really convinced Louis, however. That, and the strange, lilting music that suddenly seemed to be piping from somewhere on the other side.

"I'm gonna squeeze through," Jake said.

And that was how they'd first pierced the Veil. That was how they'd wound up in the Faerie kingdom and nearly broken a century of quiet truce between the two worlds.

It wasn't anything they'd planned. But try telling that to somebody like Manny—who, if he was lucky, had never even seen one of the Fae up close. Even Oberon, that lummox of a king of theirs, had never completely bought the boys' story.

The truth was, you weren't supposed to be able to break in. That was what the Veil was *for*.

Of course, it hadn't helped any that Jake kept going back.

"I don't need that kind of trouble here," Manny says. "You two are still, what the hell do ya call it? *Marked*."

"Relax," Louis says, already knowing the bartender won't. He's had this conversation too many times before. "It's not like *you're* in any danger. There are still pacts, treaties. There's supposed to be a barrier between our world and theirs."

"What do ya mean *supposed* to be?" Manny asks.

Yeah, Louis thinks, they always catch *that* part of it, don't they?

But hell, he isn't lying: the Veil *is* supposed to be a curtain between the two worlds. Humans on one side, the fair folk—and how they'd ever got *that* name, he doesn't know—on the other. Louis can't help it if the thing gets a little threadbare and thin in places.

He's only trespassed that one time.

"Look, I just need you to think long and hard about this," Louis tells the bartender. "Did my brother say anything else or give you any idea where he might be headed?"

"No," Manny says, "what you need is to get the hell outta here before I do something I won't regret later on."

Yeah, Louis thinks with a heavy sigh. Story of my life.

"Keep the change," he says and walks out.

§

He heads back uptown to check a couple other places where Jake might have expected to find him. Reilly's on 85th. The laundry where he worked before Jake's last visit got him fired. There's no luck anywhere, no sign of his brother, no more dumb notes. Either Jake is getting lazier or Louis is getting more predictable.

He's coming up from the subway a couple blocks from his apartment when he finally spots his brother. Jake is waiting for him on the stoop outside, smoking a cigarette—and not his first, judging by the circle of butts at his feet.

"I should've guessed," Louis says. "What happened to running?"

"What happened to *hello*?" Jake asks. A wide grin splits across his face. "Haven't seen you in months and already you start with the attitude?"

"I've just been half over town looking for you," Louis says. "While, I dunno, maybe I should've been looking over my shoulder?"

"Oh," Jake says. "So you got the note."

"Yeah. What the hell did you do?"

"First of all, it wasn't my fault. The Veil was gonna part no matter what I did to it."

"What *did* you do to it?"

"I dunno." Jake shrugs. "Just some ordinary magic. Pretty ordinary. I picked up a couple of things on the other side, you know? I thought if I could get it down just long enough, I could get both of us out this time."

"Uh huh," Louis says. "And that's what, you and the girl?" There's always some girl wherever Jake is concerned.

"Yeah," Jake says. "But instead..." He stubs the cigarette out

5

beneath his boot and shrugs again. "I mean, it's still up. The Veil's still *there*, kinda. It's just...fading fast. I wouldn't expect it'd take Oberon more than a couple of days to have it torn down completely."

"And then what? The whole Faerie army comes pouring through?"

"Yeah..." Jake considers. "Could be. Old Obie *is* still pretty pissed off. He might just do that."

Truth is, Oberon probably doesn't need much convincing, Louis thinks. You don't keep your armies on standby, ready to punch through a mystical Veil between worlds, unless deep down you're itching for some kind of fight.

And if there's one thing everybody agrees on, it's that *fighting* is definitely something the Faerie king knows how to do well.

That's not to say the Veil hasn't always been a *little* permeable, of course, even without Oberon turning his attention toward it. Every now and then, one or two of the Fae will slip through into this world, the same way Jake keeps going through the door in the woods, if they can find a shimmering tear on their side that's wide enough to let them pass. But those are isolated cases. Rumors and whispers and their grandmother's stories. Those aren't battle-hardened magical armies ready to die and kill at the angry whim of their king.

"It might not have helped that it was his daughter this time," says Jake.

"Goddamn it!" Louis says. "Jake, please tell me you did not fall for a faerie princess."

"Hey, this one's special!" Jake says. "I think you'd really like her."

"Uh huh. And where is little miss special now?"

"Well that's kind of the thing..." Jake says. "To be honest, I'm not a hundred percent sure."

"You're not what?" Louis asks. "What percentage of sure *are* you?"

"She kinda split when we got to the city. It was going great up until then, but... I dunno, she needs her space or something, says maybe we should see other people. I've bumped into her at a couple of parties downtown, but—"

"You've *bumped into her*? Just how long have you two been back in the city?"

"I dunno, maybe a week?"

"*Goddamn it*! And you're just coming to tell me about this shitstorm now?"

"I was gonna handle it," Jake says. "I thought if I could convince her to come back with me, we'd talk it out with her dad. Stitch the Veil back together or something. No harm, no foul. But turns out she's got all these other... I dunno, ideas, plans, schemes."

Louis narrows his eyes. "What kind of plans?" he asks. "What kind of schemes?"

"I dunno." Jake says. "Way I hear it, she's enrolled at NYU."

"She's—wait, what?"

"At the film school," Jake tells him. "I know, it seems kinda late in the semester to me too. And just where in hell is she supposed to be transferring from, I dunno. But hey, she wants to make movies."

His brother grins.

"I told you this one's special."

"Well clearly," Louis says. "I mean, if she dumped you."

"Wait, what? Nah, I wouldn't go that far. We're just...y'know, on a break."

"Face it, Jake. You kidnapped a faerie princess, knocked down the only thing that'd stop her lunatic father from waging another war to get her back...and then she dumped you." This time it's

Louis who grins. "Actually, that almost makes this whole damn thing worth it for me."

"Yeah, well I'm glad somebody's enjoying my heartbreak," Jake says. "Meanwhile, we've got maybe a day or two before Oberon and his crew get here and I'm running out of options."

"I wish I knew what to tell you, Jake," Louis says. "But Oberon doesn't like me any more than he does you."

"Yeah..." Jake says. "That's true." He fishes a pack of cigarettes from his jacket and shakes one loose. "Thing is, though, I think maybe I know somebody else who does."

Louis stares at his brother. "Oh no," he says. "No goddamn way."

"But we *have to*," Jake says. "You know Oberon's not just gonna *stop* once he gets Amy back."

"Who the hell is Amy?" Louis says.

"His daughter." Jake shrugs again. "It's short for Amoret. He'll use it as an excuse to burn this city to the ground, then the next city and the next. He's not what you'd call *reasonable*. But the other one? *Her*? With her we maybe got a chance."

"I don't like this one little bit," Louis says. "Frankly, I don't like *her*."

"Yeah, I know," Jake acknowledges. "But she sure likes you. And the way I see it, we got no other choice."

He lights the cigarette and takes a drag.

"We gotta go and talk with Queen Titania."

§

When they'd first trespassed into the Faerie realm that long-ago morning, Louis and Jake had been apprehended almost immediately. The same thing happened on their way back a couple of hours later, when their grandfather and the local sheriff caught the two boys stumbling out of the woods.

Louis doesn't exactly pin much hope on their cunning or their guile.

It had been a festival day that morning—one of the hundreds, as it later turned out, that were celebrated in the Faerie kingdom annually, or however it was that the Fae reckoned time. The woods on the other side of the door were strung with silver garlands, and the air had been colder, too, with the chill of early winter. Louis wasn't at all surprised by the light dusting of perfect snow already on the ground.

He and Jake stepped through the door in the tree directly into the path of a large, jubilant procession. At its head stood a trio of ghost-white riders, atop what looked at least vaguely like horses, if you didn't let your eyes stare at them too long or too closely, with a large caravan of ornamented coaches following closely behind.

Even at eleven, Louis knew this was a little outside of the norm for a Saturday morning.

"Hold!" cried a deep voice from the interior of the front coach, and suddenly the music Louis wasn't even entirely sure he'd been hearing before that was silenced. He was sure he would remember that voice, though, even if his memory shook loose everything else. The procession—if not the very woods—halted at the sound of it.

"What now, husband?" sighed a weary voice from the same coach.

"M'lord?" called back one of the riders.

"Are the whole lot of you *blind*?" the first voice asked, as an impressively towering figure, clad head to toe in silver finery, stepped from the coach. This, Louis would soon come to learn, was Oberon, the king of the faeries. "There are children on our parade route. *Human* children."

"*Really*?" asked the second voice, as another figure, dressed nearly the same, leaned her head out from the coach. "Well that *is* most unusual."

This, Louis would also come to learn, was Titania, the queen of the Faerie realm.

"Don't just stand there gawping!" Oberon spat at his riders. "Seize them already!"

Two of the riders dismounted, grabbing Louis and Jake before either of the brothers could react. They were tossed, roughly, into the back of the coach, where Louis came face to face with the queen. She regarded him closely and intently, saying nothing.

"You have disturbed our morning festivities," said Oberon, as he sat down across from them. He rapped his fist against the roof of the coach and it jolted forward. "We are most displeased with this intrusion."

"Hi there!" said Jake. He held out a hand, totally unfazed. "Jake Palmer. And you are...?"

Oberon glared. "Do not test our patience, child. You know precisely who we are, and precisely where you have strayed."

"Is this...is this *Faerie*?" Louis asked.

Titania beamed. "You recognize it, then?" she said.

"Um...just from stories," Louis answered. He wasn't quite sure he liked the appraising look that had suddenly crossed the queen's smiling face.

"Then you know that you have trespassed," Oberon said. "Your punishment for that will be swift and severe and most deservedly unpleasant."

"Now, husband," said the queen, holding up her hand, "let us not be hasty. Nor let us spoil this day of joyous celebration with idle threats."

"You mistake steely resolve for idleness, my lady," said the king.

"And you mistake the foolish innocence of youth for treachery and deceit." She turned warmly to Louis, as if they were old friends. "Speak plainly, child. Why are you here?"

"We...we found a door?" Louis ventured.

Oberon huffed. "And are you in the habit of traipsing through all doors uninvited?"

"It...it was open?"

"Such transparent deception!" growled the king. "When these are *clearly* agents of the mortal world, dispatched here to spy upon us!"

Titania laughed, though Louis took no comfort in the sound of it. There were hidden depths to that laughter, he thought, whole geographies hidden from sight and best left unexplored.

"And is stumbling blindly into a parade what passes for subterfuge among the humans, then?" asked the queen. "No, Oberon, these are frightened children who mean us no harm." She turned her smile again toward Louis and his brother. "You forget when human children were friends to our kingdom."

"And you forget what first turned that friendship sour," Oberon answered. "Or would you have us break our compacts and return to old habits?"

"So we're *not* doing introductions, then?" Jake asked, finally dropping his hand.

"We didn't mean to cause any trouble," Louis said. "If you'll just turn us around, I'm sure we can be back on our way."

"Oh no!" shouted Titania, surprising them all—even Oberon, it seemed—with her urgency. "What I mean," she said, "is that you haven't even seen any of the realm. It's most beautiful this time of year. And since you are clearly *not* spies—" she stared pointedly at the king "—you *could* stay, if for just a little while...?"

"Titania," said Oberon. "*Don't.*"

"What?" she said. "I am simply extending the warm welcome of hospitality, husband. Surely *some* of the old ways are still worth our effort."

She turned directly to Louis, still smiling.

"Now, tell me, child..." she said, "and speak without any cause for fear: what do you know about *changelings*...?"

§

"So what's this all about?" asks Amy, maybe forty minutes later. "You were kind of vague on the phone."

"Uh, yeah..." Louis says. "I just thought maybe we should talk about magical Armageddon in person, is all."

"Oh," Amy says. "So it's about my dad."

They've met up with her in Washington Square Park after they finally reached her on Jake's cell. Louis is a little surprised she picked up at all, much less agreed to meet, but maybe it helps that it was him who called and not Jake.

She *is* a little pale maybe, Louis thinks, but nothing other-worldly, and he doubts he'd have recognized her as one of the Fae at all unless Jake pointed her out.

A glamour, maybe? It's hard to tell, and he's never really had an eye for it. Either way, she doesn't look much different than any of the other college students hanging out in the park around them, even if she is the only one without streaks of green or pink in her hair.

"I don't know how much Jake's told you about when we were kids..." Louis says.

"Just the basics," says Amy. She shrugs. "But it's not like I didn't hear all about you two growing up. What Jake *didn't* say anything about was my dad starting another war."

Louis glares at his brother.

"*What*?" Jake says. "I kinda took that as *understood*." He turns to look at Amy. "I mean, have you *met* your dad?"

"I have," she says, "which is why I know asking him nicely to not burn this world to ashes probably isn't going to work."

"We were hoping you could help us convince Oberon," says Louis. "Or maybe—" He sighs. "God help us, maybe more likely Titania?"

"My *mom*?" Amy says. "I guess you could *try*. I'm not sure she's a whole lot more open-minded than my dad, though." She frowns. "You know how it is with their generation."

"They're like hundreds of centuries old," says Jake. "And they're practically *immortal*!"

"Yeah, my point exactly," says Amy. "They're kinda set in their ways. But Mom is little less 'unleash the fiery armies upon mankind,' so she probably is your safer bet."

"So you'll help us?" Louis asks.

"Sure," says Amy. "I mean, I've got a poli-sci test I'm supposed to study for on Monday, but who knows? Maybe averting a second Faerie War will get me extra credit or something."

She shrugs.

"So, where do we start?"

§

Their grandparents' house has, for several years now, been owned by the county, but for whatever reason it still stands vacant at the edge of the property. The paint is peeled, gone more gray than yellow, and thick boards cover the windows and doors. It doesn't look anything like the house they grew up in, and Louis doesn't even argue when Jake takes one good look—and then one good kick—at the front steps and says, "Poppy kinda let the place go to crap after we left, huh?"

They aren't here for the house, anyway. They're here for what's at the edge of the property, out in the woods just past it— what, for now at least, is the only open hole they know of in the Veil.

"What happened to your car?" Jake says, as the three of them leave the gravel dust of their grandparents' old driveway behind.

"I could ask you the same thing," Louis says.

"You mean that old rust heap I had like a year ago?" Jake asks. He seems honestly amused by the thought. "Nah, that thing was never mine."

"Yeah, that's kinda what I meant," Louis says. "That was *my* car. You stole it last time you were back in town."

"I did?" Jake chuckles. "Well *that* explains a lot. Still, we could've rented something. End of the world's no time to be living on a budget. We didn't even stop anyplace for dinner."

"He bought you a sandwich," Amy says.

"From a bus station vending machine," says Jake. "You have any idea how long that turkey and Swiss was probably in there?"

"It's why I didn't buy more than one," says Louis. "I figure if you croak from botulism, we've got an even chance Oberon will call us square, all debts paid."

"Very funny."

They walk a little while, Louis relying on Jake's memory of the tree and the tear, or on Amy's innate connection to the Faerie realm, to guide them. He's avoided coming back this way for almost twenty years, and the woods don't look any more inviting this evening than they did back then. The sun isn't going to stay up a whole lot longer, either, and the idea of doing this in the dark doesn't exactly thrill Louis to pieces.

"Can I ask you something?" Amy says to Louis. "I know my mom can be a little nuts sometimes, but when you mentioned her before, it seemed like maybe there was something else going on? Do you really not like her?"

Louis sighs. "It's not that," he says, "Not exactly. It's just... I think maybe she liked *me* a little too much."

"She thought he was a changeling," Jake says.

14

Amy laughs out loud. "Really?"

"Yeah," says Louis. "She did seem pretty damned convinced."

More than that, Titania had been convinced that she recognized Louis specifically, and she had wanted him to stay almost as much as Oberon had wanted the both of them gone. The whole thing had made Louis feel incredibly uncomfortable, and it was a big reason why he had never been tempted to go back.

"I don't see what the big deal is," says Jake. "So you're a changeling? It happens."

"Do you even know what a changeling is?" Louis asks.

"Sure," says Jake, "I'm not dumb. It's...well, you know."

Louis shakes his head. "How can you spend so much time over there and never learn a damn thing about the place?"

"That's what I keep saying," says Amy. "But yeah, that does sound like my mom. Changelings were kind of her thing for a while."

"Her *thing*?"

"You know, kidnapping human infants, leaving a baby Fae behind in the crib." She shrugs. "I guess everybody needs some kind of hobby."

"Well, all I know is, I didn't like it," Louis says. "I felt like we only just escaped the last time I was there."

"And we're here," says Jake.

The tree is a *lot* smaller than Louis remembers it. It doesn't look half as imposing as the one that's since then sprouted up in his memories. It's shorter, even, than a lot of the other nearby trees in the surrounding woods, and Louis wonders for a minute if maybe Jake's just too stubborn to admit that he's gotten them all lost.

But sure enough, when Louis looks a little closer, there at the base of the tree is the door, the slender rip in the Veil that leads to another world.

"It's a little narrow, isn't it?" he asks.

"Really?" Jake says. "I was thinking it's maybe a little wider than it was a week ago." He looks at Amy, as if for confirmation, then back at Louis with a shrug. "Of course, it'll still probably pinch you at the shoulders."

Louis has no doubt. The door itself doesn't look any bigger than it did when he was eleven...although it does look a lot more like a *door*, come to think of it. You don't have to glance at it from the corner of your eye to see the golden sheen around the edges, the square outline where Faerie magic meets the wood. Maybe that's the Veil getting weaker, the two worlds slipping into each other—Louis doesn't know. But he knows he has to follow Jake and Amy when the two of them quietly crawl through.

"So what exactly *is* the plan?" Amy asks when they're in the summery, sunlit woods on the other side.

"Well," says Jake, "it may surprise you both to learn, but I *have* given this some thought."

He grabs a stick from the ground and starts tracing unintelligible symbols and lines into the dirt.

"The way I see it, now that we've snuck back across, we need to evade capture by any sentries Oberon's got posted—here and here—hike maybe ten miles across open terrain to the royal palace—here—talk our way into the inner court, where we demand an audience with Titania, her majesty the faerie queen, and then—"

"Uh huh," Louis says. "Or we *could* just get captured again."

He points at the path that leads away from the tree. He's pretty sure it isn't *all* of Oberon's army that's standing there, but a sizable percentage of it has them surrounded.

"Oh," says Jake. He grins and waves at the faerie troops. "Hi, fellas. Um, take us to your leader?"

§

"Tell me why I should not execute you both where you stand," roars the Faerie king.

If anything, this is a warmer reception than Louis expected.

Oberon is taller than he remembers, more towering and imposing. Although that might have something to do with the genuine majesty of the Faerie court, which Louis only saw in passing the last time around, or with the dozens of soldiers still pointing very sharp swords in their general direction.

"We didn't *have* to come back," Louis says. "We could've run."

"Wait a minute," Jake says, "we *could've* run?"

"And yeah, I know there's probably nowhere you couldn't have found us," Louis adds, ignoring his brother, "but do you really want to start another war? Over *this*?"

From his throne, Oberon glares.

Most of what Louis actually knows about the Fae still comes from books, the kind he read without much enthusiasm back in grade school, or from their grandmother's stories. He knows the two realms used to intermingle all the time, rubbed shoulders for centuries without any need for a Veil between them. It's never been clear to him why all of that changed. All he knows is, Oberon could be capricious, quick-tempered, even brutal—and that was *before* he'd ever met Louis' brother, Jake.

"Is that what *you* want?" Louis asks, turning to face the throne at Oberon's right. "My lady?"

Titania smiles. "Husband," the queen of Faerie says, "perhaps the human child is right. What profit is there in more costly bloodshed?"

"We have a contract," the king shouts, "and we *will* have restitution! Our daughter was betrothed to another!"

"Oh geez, Dad" says Amy, "not this whole arranged marriage thing again. I was never getting wed to Peaseblossom of all people, and you know it!"

Jake smirks. "*Peaseblossom*?"

"Oh please," says Amy. "What was the name of that girl you dated right before me? *Courtney*?"

"Fair enough," says Jake.

"Oberon," interjects Titania, "is our daughter truly to forfeit her happiness, and the world she has chosen truly to burn, simply for the sake of a *contract*?" She smiles again and places an ice-white hand atop his. "After all, what is a contract to a *king*?"

"There are still rules," Oberon huffs. "Even for kings. As you well know, it demands an exchange. We cannot simply let them leave, unless—"

"Unless another remains in her place," Titania finishes for him. She nods at the sage wisdom of this, then stares directly and pointedly at Louis. "Perhaps the human child...?"

"Wait, what?" Louis says.

"Mom!" yells Amy. "He is *not* a changeling, for Pete's sake!"

"I'm sure I don't know *what* you mean," Titania tells her daughter.

"Besides, you stopped doing that like a hundred years ago! Just how old do you think the two of them *are*?"

"Well, I..." Titania seems to squint at Louis, considering. "How many centuries *do* these humans live?"

Amy rolls her eyes. "You see what I mean about set in their ways?" she says to Louis.

"Wait," says Jake, "when you say an exchange... Does that mean one of *us* has to get married to Peaseblossom?"

Oberon stares, says nothing. "No," he sighs at last, "I suppose there *is* something to satisfy all needs here, both magic and mortal." He waves a hand and the army around them stands down.

"Tell me, human," he says to Louis, who braces himself for whatever madness will come next. "How would you like a change in *employment*?"

§

"So that's it?" Manny asks, when Louis finds himself a couple of weeks later back in the bar. "'Think but this and all is mended'?"

When Louis raises an eyebrow, the bartender adds, "What? I can't have read a book? What I mean is, guy just offers you a *job*?"

Louis laughs. "Yeah, that's pretty much what happened."

Manny wasn't too happy to see Louis at first. A few harsh words and a near-miss with a baseball bat behind the bar might have been exchanged before Louis had a chance to explain everything.

Of all the trouble Louis had seen coming, suddenly getting named ambassador to the Faerie realm hadn't been anywhere on the list. But that was exactly what Oberon suggested.

"We have been too long out of the mortal world," said the Faerie king. "It is perhaps time we remedied that."

It'll mean traveling back and forth between the two worlds a lot more than Louis maybe wants. But the Veil isn't getting stitched back together anytime soon. Oberon had to admit it was going to fall no matter what, and they're going to need somebody to make sure the truce doesn't fall with it.

Hell, at least it beats laundry work.

He'd wondered why not Jake, of course. His brother *is* the one who's kept going back over the years, who's shown some aptitude or talent, however misplaced, for faerie magic. And neither one of them are changelings; Louis likes to think they've at least put *that* matter to bed. So why not his brother?

But Oberon just stared at him. "Seriously?" he'd said. "*Jake*?"

"It's possible," Louis said. "I mean, of the two of us, he seems like maybe the more obvious choice."

"Yes, but... *Jake*?"

"Fair enough," said Louis.

Stories like this usually end in weddings or death, he thinks. Or at least that's the old saying. Or at least it is in fairy tales. But he guesses that since this is only half a fairy tale, at best, a canceled wedding and a new job will have to suffice.

"And the girl?" Manny asks.

"She shows real promise," Louis says. "At least that's what her professors say. And it's pretty impressive, considering they don't even *have* movies on the other side."

"Nah?" Manny asks. "Not even, like, cartoons or nothin'?"

"Not even cartoons," Louis says. "It's a brave new world."

"I'm still not sure I believe it, though," the bartender says. "Just like that? Your brother breaks down the Veil between worlds, nearly starts another war, but it's all one big happy ending?"

"Looks that way," Louis says. He smiles. "They talk a big game, and they've got the muscle to play it, if it comes to that. But in their heart, or whatever it is that a faerie's got, there's a soft spot for humanity."

He takes a sip of his beer.

"It's why they let us go that first time," he says. "Why they kept chasing Jake out every time he snuck back, but it never turned into anything serious."

"The war, threatening another—that wasn't *serious*?" Manny asks.

"Not for the Fae," Louis says. He shrugs again. Honestly, he's not even sure this wasn't Oberon's plan all along. "They've got some unusual ways of doing things, is all."

"I'll bet," Manny says, like a man grateful he'll never have to find out.

"So anyway," says Louis, "that's what I've been up to lately. Now how about some eggs?"

Fred Coppersmith's fiction has appeared occasionally in places like *Bourbon Penn*, *Etherea Magazine*, and previously in *Stupefying Stories*, among others. He lives and writes in New York, where he also edits and publishes the quarterly online SFF magazine *Kaleidotrope*. You can find him online, if you're so inclined, at unreality.net.

The Demolition Job

By Neva Bryan

IT HAD RAINED ALL DAY. Alice tried to peer through a window, but grime and ribbons of stormwater hid the outside world and darkened the room. Out there languished the remains of an old coal-mining town that had died a slow, lingering death after the company shut down in the 1970s. Residents had moved away a few at a time, and now there were only two families left. Their houses were on the other end of the dead town, far from the building where Alice stood.

"Mommy, I don't like it here."

"I know, Sweetie." Alice crouched next to her five-year-old daughter and rubbed her nose against Sadie's. She hesitated to touch her with her gloved hand. "It's not a nice place."

That was an understatement.

They were on the third floor of a four-story building that the coal company had erected in the early 1900s. It had served as a field office until the company shut down. Now vacant for nearly forty years, the building would be demolished come summer.

The county Industrial Development Authority had hired Alice and three other people to empty the building of its contents: furniture, filing cabinets, papers, and other detritus. The IDA director had asked them to set aside documents that might have potential historical value, but so far, none of them had done that.

There's ain't jack worth a shit here, Alice thought. She stood and stretched her back. *Except for my Sadie.*

"Go sit on that blanket I laid out for you. Watch where you step. Don't take your gloves off, and don't touch anything, you hear?"

"Okay, Mommy." Sadie returned to one of the few clear spaces in the cavernous room and plopped down with a grunt. Dust rose around her. The yellow kitchen gloves that Alice had rolled down to her daughter's little elbows glowed in the light of her headlamp. Sadie's red bandana puffed in and out as she breathed. Alice's throat tightened. She swallowed hard and turned her head.

Doug leaned on the shovel he'd been using to pick up refuse. "If they was to see her here, you'd catch hell for it."

"I don't have a choice. Her meemaw died last year, and my piece-of-shit ex skipped town before that, so I got no family. No money for a babysitter."

The nursing home where Alice had worked for three years had laid her off six months ago, along with three other nurse's aides.

"Besides," she said, "nobody in their right mind would come in here unless they were desperate for a paycheck."

Doug laughed. "Well, that's us. Desperate and not in our right minds."

He was a skinny fellow with a mullet, and his eyes were two different colors. This job was the only one he could get that didn't require a drug test. Alice knew this because she had heard the other two crew members whispering about it that morning.

She didn't care. He was a hard worker. He hadn't stopped for a break every few minutes like the others. Neither had she, even though she'd been craving a cigarette for hours. She was down to her last three. She wouldn't be buying any more.

Feed my habit or feed my kid. It was an easy decision. *I'd kill for her if I had to*, she thought.

Now they stood in the center of a large room on the third floor and stared at their progress. The light of their headlamps pierced the shadows and lit upon piles of letters and accounting ledgers that were swollen with moisture. Doug and Alice had swept and shoveled all the paper and books into the center of the room. The stink of mold and mouse poop wafted toward them whenever the pile shifted.

"We need to bag it up," she told him.

"I don't know why they don't just burn this building to the ground with all this stuff in it. That'd be easier," Doug said.

She shrugged. "Maybe it's a law that it has to be empty first. I guess they want to make sure there's no hazardous materials."

The IDA had purchased most of the old town. Once the land was cleared, including the abandoned houses and buildings like this one, they would build shell buildings suitable for manufacturing. Developers hoped to attract new employers to the economically depressed area.

Doug grinned. "That's a joke. What could be more hazardous than that gob pile out there?"

He pointed to the window even though the mountain of coal waste he referred to wasn't visible from that side of the building.

When Alice shrugged, he said, "You grew up here, just like I did. You know as well as I do that they ruined our creeks with gob runoff. Mercury. Sulfur. Killed all the fish. God only knows what it does to other animals. To people."

"Take it easy. I ain't the one done did it."

"Sorry." Doug rested his hands on his hips and looked around the room. "Dang. What happened to that box of trash bags?"

"I think Chuck took them downstairs to the basement. Never bothered to bring them back."

The cleaning crew had spent the better part of the morning attacking their task, but after lunch, the two coworkers disappeared. "They must have ditched us," she told Doug.

He agreed. "Maybe they don't need the dough as much as I do." He sighed, then started across the room. "I'll be back in a few minutes."

She called out to him, "Watch those stairs!"

The steps were warped from water damage, rotting in places. *God, if Child Protective Services finds out I had Sadie in this deathtrap...*

Between the rotten floors and the rodents, it would be easy for a kid to get hurt in here.

She decided Doug was right. The building just needed to be burned to the ground.

She called to Sadie, "You doing okay over there?"

"Uh-huh."

Sadie was the most agreeable kid Alice had ever known.

It's a good thing, considering the life she's got born into.

Tired, Alice crouched and rested her arms on her thighs. She didn't want to sit on any of the furniture, as it looked unsteady and filthy. The floor was even worse. So she rested in a hunched position and tried to ignore how dirty her exposed skin felt.

She pulled her cigarette lighter from her back pocket, then shoved it back into place. *Let's see how long I can wait.*

The room was much darker now without Doug's headlamp. Alice closed her eyes and listened to the rain hit the window. The wind picked up, and a loose board clattered against the building. Someone dragged a wet quilt across the floor.

She shined her headlamp towards her daughter. Sadie hadn't moved. She was playing with a naked Barbie doll, the thick blanket folded beneath her. Alice scanned the area around her daughter, worried that a rat might be lurking in the shadows.

Finally, she closed her eyes again and listened to the strange sound. Now she could make out that it was coming from the second floor. Maybe Amber and Chuck didn't leave after all. They must be working right below us.

She stood and walked across the room to the doorway. "Don't move, Sadie honey. I'll be right back."

She trudged to the end of the hallway and peered down the

stairwell. No light flashed from anyone else's headlamps. Are they working in the dark?

"Hello?"

The dragging sound stopped.

"Amber? Chuck? What are you guys doing?"

A pale, glistening face peered up at her from the stairwell. Alice jerked back, heart rat-a-tatting faster than hard rain on a tin roof. After a moment, she crept forward.

There was nothing there.

This place is getting to me.

When she laughed, the stained walls absorbed the sound. Alice hurried back to Sadie. As she walked around the pile of rotting paper, something dark scurried from within it and disappeared into the shadows.

"Shit!"

"Rat. There's a whole bunch of the filthy bastards in the basement."

Screaming, Alice whirled and found Doug standing in the doorway. She hadn't heard him come up the stairs.

"You about scared the shit out of me!"

"Sorry." He looked uneasy. He tossed the box of garbage bags onto the floor in front of the papers. "Well, Amber and Chuck ain't in the basement. Unless they're lost down there. It's the biggest basement I ever saw. Piled full of junk!"

"They're on the second floor. I heard them moving around a few minutes ago."

"Mommy, I'm hungry."

"Hang on, Sweetie." Alice pulled a package of peanut butter crackers from her fanny pack and took it to her daughter. "Pull your gloves off before you eat these, then put them right back on, okay?"

Doug grabbed an industrial-strength garbage bag and began to shove papers into it. Alice did the same. They worked quickly and quietly. When the light from her headlamp illuminated Doug's face, it exaggerated his features. His eyes looked like two caverns, deep in shadows.

"This'd be a lot easier if we had a dumpster stationed below the windows," Alice said. "We wouldn't have to bother with bagging up so much of this shit."

Doug didn't respond. He walked to the doorway and peered down the hallway. After he did it a couple more times, Alice grew irritated.

We're losing time. We'll be here for weeks.

His pacing made her nervous, too.

"Will you stop that?"

"Sorry." He didn't move from the doorway. "Thought I heard something."

"I told you. Amber and Chuck are on the second floor."

It sounded like their coworkers were getting some real work done now. The wet sliding sound started again, this time accompanied by an occasional thumping noise. Alice pictured the two of them dragging trash bags across the floor and tossing them down the stairwell.

"Are you sure that's them?" Doug asked.

Alice paused in the act of tying off a full trash bag. "Who else would it be, Doug? We're the only four working here. You think they hired someone else to work, and nobody bothered to tell us?"

He raised his shoulders, then turned back to the hallway. "They ain't as talkative as they were this morning. They were chattering up a storm before lunch."

Alice thought about that as she finished tying the bag. *They're probably just tired. I know I am.*

"Hey," Doug said. "I'm going to go check on them. Be right back."

"Hurry up."

As soon as Doug left the room, Alice walked to the window again. The rain was coming down harder now. It would be night soon. She pulled off her thick gloves and slapped them against her thigh.

"We're almost done, Sadie."

"Okay." The sound of crinkling cellophane followed.

Footsteps sounded on the stairs, followed by a loud crash. Heart sinking, Alice pictured a step giving way with Doug. Dropping her gloves, she hurried out of the room.

Light shined upward from the stairwell. When she reached the end of the hall, she saw that the stairs were intact. A headlamp lay on the top step. Doug wasn't visible.

"Hey. Are you okay?"

When he didn't answer, she moved to the top step and picked up the headlamp. It was wet with something black. Alice cried in disgust, dropping it.

She descended another step. "Doug?"

Soft movement below.

She stepped down once more and found Doug. His body was in shadow, but his face was all too clear. Alice gasped.

His wide-open eyes looked like polished stones.

His mouth was open, too. Something the color of raw shrimp filled it. Alice gaped at it when she realized it was a grey hand reaching out from the shadows. It glistened in the light of her headlamp as it moved to and fro, exploring the interior of the man's mouth. The hand curled into a fist; then it snapped back. Doug's head made a *thunk* sound against the step.

The hand's fat fingers clutched a bloody pink flap. *Tongue*, she thought stupidly.

That's Doug's tongue.

The hand withdrew into the shadows with its prize. There was a noise like nothing she had ever heard before. All she could think of was a gang of kids slurping buttermilk through straws. Alice gagged.

Doug's face disappeared into the shadows. Something…some things…dragged him down the stairs. His head thumped dully against the steps…once…twice…three times…then the slurping sound resumed. Alice turned and ran down the hallway to the room where they had been working.

Sadie was not on her blanket.

"Sadie? Where are you?" Moldy furniture and the bloated pile of paper flashed crazily in the light of Alice's headlamp as she looked around the space.

"Over here." The girl was behind her at the doorway. "I heard a noise, and I got scared."

"It's okay. Take my hand. We're leaving. Right now."

"What is it, Mommy? Where's Doug?" Sadie's voice pitched high like it did when she was getting ready to cry.

"Nothing, baby. Don't cry. Just try to stay real quiet and do what I tell you, okay?"

Without waiting for an answer, Alice dragged her daughter into the hallway.

There was a stairwell at the far end of the hall. She prayed this one was clear of whatever had gotten hold of Doug on the other side. They were halfway down the first flight of stairs when she remembered how rotten the steps were. Alice forced herself to slow down but was still out of breath when they reached the second-floor landing.

Out of the corner of her eye, she caught movement. Things were crawling slowly, stealthily down the second story hallway toward the stairs. They were grey…glistening as if coated with some kind of mucous. They were the size of men, but not human.

How could they possibly be human?

Puffy with decay, their flesh flaked off as they moved. The scabs oozed a liquid dark as coal. There were indentations in the tissue where eyes should be. These were the things that made that terrible slurping sound.

Sadie shrieked. "Monsters! Monsters!"

Alice hoisted her daughter up onto her hip and continued down the stairs to the first floor. There was a door here, but when she tried to push through it, nothing happened. She set her shoulder against it and shoved, but it barely moved. Then she remembered seeing Amber and Chuck piling furniture at the end of the hallway. They must have blocked the door.

There were soft thumps on the stairs above her. Sadie started to cry, a low hiccupping sound in her mother's ear. Alice cupped her face with one hand. "It'll be okay. I promise you."

She hesitated, not wanting to go downstairs farther. That was the basement. She hadn't worked in there and didn't know if there was a back way out of it.

Suddenly one of the things dropped from above and landed right next to her, wiggling like a maggot. She jumped away from it and stumbled down the stairs, praying no other furniture or trash would obstruct their path.

The basement door hung crooked on its hinges. Its bottom scraped the floor when she tried to open it. Alice set Sadie on her feet and shoved her against the wall next to the door. "Don't move!"

She put her butt against the door, braced her feet, and pushed as hard as she could. The door opened partially. She had just enough space to squeeze herself through it. Once on the other side, she reached through the opening and grabbed Sadie. After pulling her daughter through, she pressed herself against the door. It didn't close all the way.

If she hadn't been wearing the headlamp, they would have

been in complete darkness. As it was, she could only see a few feet in front of them. She clutched Sadie's shoulder, and the girl cried out, "You're hurting me!"

"I'm sorry. Sorry, baby." Alice loosened her grip.

She nudged her daughter forward a few steps, then stopped to listen. There was a scrabbling sound around the edges of the door behind them. They moved farther away from it.

Like the rest of the building, the basement was piled full of rubbish. Broken furniture. Rusty tools. Old mining equipment. Something scuttled from the darkness, knocking over a stack of magazines. A possum appeared in their path, its thick pink tail twitching. It hissed at them but was suddenly overwhelmed by a mass of fat, grey bodies.

The creatures clambered over each other as they reached for the possum. The animal tore at their hands, ripping pieces of putrid flesh, but that didn't slow them. Even though the gaping holes that must have been their mouths didn't appear to have teeth, the possum squealed when they fell on top of it. Then it was quiet except for that slurping sound, which echoed in Alice's head.

A sob escaped Sadie, and the monsters turned toward them. They lifted their heads as if sniffing the air.

Maybe they're blind, Alice thought. Indentations for eyes.

But the things seemed to be able to smell them—their terror.

Or our blood.

They bumped against each other, moving in Alice's direction. Sadie turned and buried her face in her mother's stomach.

The door creaked open behind Alice. She glanced back and saw soft fingers, like grey worms, trying to push the door open.

Panic collared her throat, constricting it.

She scanned their immediate surroundings. Nearby a rusty piece of rebar lay across a discarded sofa. Leaning across Sadie, Alice grabbed the metal bar and turned to hack the hand coming through the crack in the door. Two of its swollen fingers broke off and dropped to the floor. Black droplets beaded up at the finger stumps, and the hand withdrew.

Alice kneeled and told Sadie to jump on her back. "Hold on tight around my neck. Don't let go, baby!"

She could hardly breathe in Sadie's death grip, but she didn't ask her to loosen it. When she stood, she found the things…monsters, Sadie called them… much closer. She thrust the rebar at the nearest one, then recoiled when its face came apart, its flesh clinging to the metal bar. The other creatures crawled over the injured one and began to tear it apart.

Alice felt her mind give a little then as if trying to fold in on itself.

Keep your shit together!

While they were cannibalizing one of their own, Alice retrieved her lighter from her pocket and used it to set fire to the sofa. The fabric was damp, and she was afraid it wouldn't burn, but luck was with her. Flames began to lick the back of the couch.

She watched the fire spread for a quick moment, then grabbed a blazing cushion and threw it onto the pile of creatures as they ate. They burned quickly, their flesh sizzling, their black blood dripping onto the floor. They made no noise but writhed on the floor as their skin began to char.

"Mommy! Monsters are getting in! They're getting in!" Sadie screamed so loud that Alice thought her ear might bleed.

She turned slowly, her tread heavy with the weight of her daughter on her back. Bloated hands were reaching through the door, pushing it open. Without hesitation, Alice jabbed the fingers with the rebar. When they pulled away from the door, she shoved it almost shut.

Panting, she staggered around and reached for another flaming couch cushion. Fire seared her skin. She squealed in pain and patted her hand against her leg.

Grabbing the cushion, she used it as a shield, holding it in front of them as she stumbled around the burning monsters. Even on fire, they continued to devour their downed companion. When she felt something moist clamp onto her ankle, she shook it off and heaved Sadie higher onto her back. She threw the flaming cushion at it.

Without waiting to see if she had set this one ablaze, Alice limped forward, weaving between the junk and trash. She prayed there was a second door or a window somewhere in the vast expanse of the basement. She couldn't bear the thought of Sadie burning to death in this hellish space.

Orange light flickered around them. Magazines and papers crackled in flames. Smoke rose to the ceiling. Coughing, Alice stumbled on. Her back was slick with her sweat and Sadie's. Black spots floated in her vision.

To her right, the basement wall was disintegrating. Part of the gob pile behind the building filled the space, a landslide of black waste. Grey bodies wriggled out of the gob and into the room.

Alice blinked away tears as she veered away from them. When she reached the far side of the basement, she scooted along the wall, her hands flat against its slimy surface.

She lost her footing and fell sideways. Sadie tumbled over her shoulders, into a pile of coal. Her eyes were closed. She didn't move when her mother shook her.

Alice looked across the basement and saw that the creatures had managed to get the door open. They were crawling over and around the burning ones, their slack mouths smacking as they moved toward her. Those crawling out of the encroaching gob pile joined them.

Cursing, she climbed to her feet and grabbed Sadie. She slung her daughter over her shoulder like she was a sack of dog food.

The area where she stood was the bottom of a coal chute. Old buildings like this, equipped with coal furnaces, had fuel delivered down a chute. Whoever operated the furnace would shovel coal directly into it.

Alice crawled up the pile of coal, balancing herself with one hand while she hung on to Sadie with the other. She clambered up the chute's incline and shoved at the double doors. They were locked but so rotten that they gave way with the lock still intact on one side.

Alice crawled through splintered boards and stumbled out of the basement. She ran several yards away from it, raindrops stinging her face. When she turned, she saw black smoke roiling through the doors, bittering the air. The coal was on fire.

She lowered Sadie to the ground and swiped her hair back from her face. The girl opened her eyes but seemed to look beyond Alice. She wondered if her daughter was in shock, until she said, "The monsters are watching us."

Turning, Alice squinted at the bright flames. Fire licked the first-floor windows now. It had burned through the ceiling of the basement.

She raised her eyes—hideous monstrosities massed at the second- and third-floor windows. And below, one of the creatures was squirming its way through the coal chute doors.

Alice picked up Sadie and cradled her to her chest as she ran to her car.

After she buckled Sadie into the back seat, she crawled into the front and locked the doors. Only then did she get the nerve to look at the building again.

It was burning furiously.

The gob pile towered behind it. It was on fire, too.

Alice thrust the car into gear and spun it into the middle of the road. As she fled, she spotted more bodies worming their way out of the pile. The dark gob was giving birth to a thousand obscenities.

Neva Bryan's work, which includes more than 60 short stories, poems, and essays, is published in literary journals, online magazines, and anthologies. Selected publications include *Weirdbook Magazine, Quail Bell Magazine, Minding Nature, We All Live Downstream: Writings about Mountaintop Removal, Oh Reader, The Bark,* and the *Anthology of Appalachian Writers*. In addition, Neva is the author of two novels, a children's picture book, and a collection of short stories and poems. She lives in the Virginia mountains with her husband and their dog, Smiley Cyrus.

Tin Lizzi

By J. L. Royce

"AND *NOW*—LEADING HER TEAM INTO PLAY HERE AT THE NEW WOLLONGONG CIVIC DOME, the Beihai Bombers' league-leading *driver*, forty-nine kilos of AI-infused *excitement*—Tin Lizzi!"

Lizzi leapt in from the visiting team pen, across the dome and onward, running up the opposite curved wall and kicking off into a somersault. She spun in slow motion, once, twice, hanging in the low gravity, pulling in her legs to whirl madly, black braid whipping through the air, a spinning yellow blur floating slowly to the floor. At the last moment she extended her legs to land, rotation carrying her into a run: her signature entry. She halted, heart pounding, tensely erect, then flung her arms overhead, signing left-handed her trademark gesture: *Play*.

Excitement overflowed her body, filling the dome. It could mean *I wanna run I wanna pee I wanna sex*—but right now it meant: *Play*.

The audience, in the real and the mix, erupted at the air ballet move. Even the local New Wollongong fans approved of the cocky young woman in the yellow and black clingsuit. With a whoop, she summoned her three teammates onto the court. They bounced in, huddled a moment, and arranged themselves in an arc to face the goal: a shimmering ring in the mix, midway across the court, rotating slowly.

The Whirlwind entered, all at once, four players cartwheeling across the floor, splitting left and right, racing up the dome wall to spin and land together, sapphire uniforms gleaming in the dome's glare. Most of the live crowd burst into applause at the introduction of their captain, Long Scythe. Beyond the dome walls, the larger virtual audience, mostly Beihai, began chanting *Bombers*, to drown out their rivals.

Lizzi stepped forward, extending her hand even as Long did. He was taller, and as lean as she. She'd played him many times, and outside the court, they were as close to friends as she had.

"If you win, I'll let you have it tonight, *meimei* …" he teased, dark eyes amused. "When *I* win…"

They'd sexed it up a few times, and might again, but right now there were more important things to think about. Liz grinned, slapped his hand hard and signed an obscene reply that left him laughing as he retreated to his line. Lizzi bounced back to her own team's position.

Her entire future could depend upon this game.

The teams faced each other across the base of the arena, the goal midway between them. The largest pressurized dome in the hemisphere was filled to capacity: a victory in itself. The crowds quieted in anticipation: bleachers in the real to left and right, and crowds in the mix appearing ahead and behind them.

The goal assumed colors: blue on one side, yellow on the other, still idling slowly above their heads. Lizzi's hands twitched at her side, her left absently signing *Fight*.

The klaxon blew, and the ball fell in the real from the top of the dome, neon green, down through the space occupied by the goal to hit the floor and bounce toward the Bombers.

Lizzi glanced up: the goal had frozen the moment the ball hit, with blue facing them. She flung herself across the court, two impossibly long strides taking her into position facing the golden side of the goal. Meanwhile, one of her forwards—Cash, very tall and very black—intercepted the ball, only to be swarmed by three of the Whirlwinds. He jumped one-legged to a side, his other leg landing and leveraging off the curved wall, rocketing over the attackers. His pass to Lizzi was true—but didn't get past Long.

The Whirlwind driver couldn't take possession but tipped it away, eliciting a roar of approval from the home crowd; but his teammates couldn't capitalize on his move, as a Bomber regained control. And so it went: the teams were well-matched, and the first of three periods ended scoreless.

Considering her bench, Lizzi rotated Cash out and Nooshin in, the former winded after repeated runs across the dome to harry the opposition and intercept the ball.

Play proceeded into the second period after a quick break, with the goal remaining in default mode. Then opportunity arrived around the middle of the period.

Long is favoring his left foot.

It was the voice Lizzi had lived with since childhood, the voice first heard as the lonely months in hospital dragged on. The AI had introduced itself as 'Molly'.

Liz had been wondering when she would get into the game.

Thanks, Liz signed, hand twitching slightly against her leg.

She scrutinized the Whirlwind's driver during the next skirmish and quickly confirmed Molly's observation. It was subtle: his moves from the left were slightly slower—almost...*regretful*. Then she waited for a chance to use it.

From a melee, Nooshin wrestled away the ball. The Whirlwind coverage kept her from attempting a pass directly to Lizzi, but the petite forward bounced into the air and passed the ball over to a Bomber guard, Cutie. The tall blond looked at Lizzi.

Signing her intent, the captain catapulted herself to Long's right. He responded a fraction of a second too late, and Liz neatly caught her guard's pass, flipping the ball cleanly through the golden goal.

The buzzer sounded, the crowd roared in pleasure or pain, the ball fell dead. Liz did a mid-air spread-eagle, slowly descending, and her teammates bounced across the dome to slap hands and hoot as they passed her.

The goal began oscillating again, and both teams lined up on the floor, sides reversed, waiting for the next ball to drop.

Well done, Molly whispered inside Lizzi's head, and the girl signed back, *And you*.

The color announcers, an ex-player and a sports chat-bot, were nattering on about Liz and the legitimacy of augmentation in sports. The bot pointed out that, were it not for the AI integrated into her premotor cortex and SMA, Lizzi wouldn't have been able to walk, much less compete.

The Whirlwind played a more defensive game, holding the Bombers to their single goal but failing to score themselves. The period ended; and as the trailing team, the Whirlwind had the choice of goal for the final period. The four huddled briefly, and then Long addressed the dome.

"Whirlwind chooses...Choker!" He grinned across at Lizzi.

Bring it, she signed back at him, hand outstretched. She projected a cocky attitude, but her eyes narrowed, considering, as the teams retreated to their pens.

"Gonna be a long-ball game," Cutie predicted, wiping the sweat from his angular face.

Lizzie signed *Yes*, and considered her teammates. She chose Cherry: no taller than herself, the girl with the tightly curled cap of scarlet hair had uncanny accuracy in long throws. The redhead got to her feet and began stretching.

Nodding at Nooshin, Liz signed *Rest*, and considered the other players. She signed *Later* before turning to grab a bulb of water, draining it greedily.

The crowd in the real was using the break to buy more Titan Orange, the local ale. A local school group's dance performance was wrapping up. Lizzi recalled her years in ballet, cut short by a grim diagnosis. She clenched her left hand, then tossed aside the bulb. Molly intervened.

Peace. Be the river, not the rock.

Fug. Off. Lizzi signed to herself, and Cutie's eyebrows went up. He didn't need Sign to understand the captain's expression. Liz shook her head at the tall guard.

Not you, she signed. He reached down to rub the side of her head, the U-shaped craniotomy scar. "For luck." The team had a superstitious fascination with her back-story, and she made no effort to hide it.

Lucky. You. she agreed. *Maybe later.* She—Molly—swiveled *their* hips, and Cutie snorted.

The klaxon sounded; the teams formed up; the crowd quieted, as the last wandering audience members resumed their seats. The goal colors oscillated, and the ball fell.

It bounced to the Bombers, but a Whirlwind forward dove across the dome and pitched it, double-handed, back to her teammates. Lizzi emphatically signed, *Off. Sides!*—but the AI referee, analyzing a dozen video streams in real-time, saw nothing wrong.

All this period, Long had been playing Lizzi one-on-one, blocking her every move. With the advantage of height and strength, it was an impasse; but the Bomber captain had an advantage: knowledge.

Long was too close to the goal. Though his pitch was good, the target contracted to barely larger than the ball. Lizzi leapt up even as Long recovered and watched for a goal. The ball touched the margin: *out*.

Lizzi faked left, then threw herself right, and saw the slight delay in Long's reaction. The Whirlwind captain made a visible effort despite his pain, lunging after her with a leap that would have easily covered her—had he reacted faster.

Lizzi had the ball right in front of the goal, which had relaxed to full width again – but she passed it back to Cherry, who lingered near the wall. The long-shot specialist jumped to meet the ball, then took her time, the other players out of range, to throw a slow pitch arcing high into space and above the Whirlwind defense. The ball drifted into the dilated goal.

The crowd screamed, approval and pain in equal measures, and Lizzi howled in victory, signing, *Sweet*, to her teammates.

Long gave her a rueful smile as the Bombers ran down the clock. The game was over, and her teammates screamed in approval.

Well done, Molly remarked. *Knowledge is worthless unless it is applied.*

Molly tended to substitute pontification for feeling.

Good moves, Lizzi signed back. *Thanks.*

It was all a balance between chance and skill. Chance gave her a childhood glioblastoma that should have killed her, but the surgeons' skill gave her a synthetic motor cortex and an AI to operate it. Chance put her in physical therapy where she could meet recovering roundball players, but the implant had turned her into a formidable player.

Whether or not chance would favor them this time, Lizzi planned to be prepared. And roundball wasn't the only reason she wanted to reach Earth…

She joined her jubilant team in the locker room.

§

"Win three of the next four and it's Luna for us!" Cherry had slipped off her uniform in preparation for a bag shower and was bouncing in slow-mo, tall and naked.

"Don't jinx it!" Nooshin replied, removing her clingsuit.

Cherry grabbed her, swinging her around one-armed, floating.

"No jinx as long as we've got our lucky star," she countered, passing her other arm around Lizzi.

Stink, you! Lizzi signed in protest. Laughing, Cherry landed them and headed for the row of bags in the corner.

"As long as they let Lizzi play," Cutie said, looking in his locker for some clean clothes.

It was a sobering thought, and Nooshin glowered at him for dampening the mood.

"I'm just saying, plenty of people think letting somebody like her play championship ball would ruin the game."

"'Like her'?"

Lizzi realized Molly was massaging their left hand, cramped from the stress.

Cutie raised his hands. "Come on; you know what I mean—a binary. The League will have to rule on her. Nobody trusts *haute* augments, much less one walking around with an AI in her head."

"Nobody?" Nooshin advanced on him.

Try to relax, the AI said to Lizzi. *The game is over.*

All her emotions were relegated to her left hand; she could rage at her body to react, but Molly could only convey so much, so that appendage bore the brunt of emotions. Lizzi raised it.

Enough, she signed. *Need sponsors too. Just*—Lizzi struggled to find the words—*just play hard.*

The pair separated. Lizzi palmed her locker and fingered open the sweat-soaked uniform, which fell away around her feet. She stepped out and tossed it along with her panties into the laundry, then took a towel from the stack and waited for a shower bag to free up.

We should sex, Molly suggested.

Why? She signed, fingers dancing on her bare thigh.

It will help you to relax, focus.

Who?

It doesn't matter to me, Molly replied.

Lizzi thought of Long Scythe, but didn't want to deal with his roundball fixation tonight. A tap on her shoulder interrupted her reverie.

"Hey! Shower, or not? You're holding up the line." Nooshin stepped around the captain and tossed her towel on a hook. "You're coming out with us, aren't you? But shower first—*please.*" Noosh's dark eyes held her gaze. "Want to share?" she offered.

Lizzi smiled and nodded, then pulled the girl over and kissed her. The damp chill of Noosh's body, the smell of her sweat and sex, made Molly purr, somewhere in the body they shared.

Nooshin climbed into a free bag and waved the captain over. Lizzi tossed her towel and stepped in, pulling up the zipper. The bag inflated, needle sprays erupting from every direction. It was cramped, but they were both petite and playful, and enjoyed the long shower.

§

The bars, brothels, and parlors were bustling along the corridor called the Combat Zone. All the big out-system towns had a place to be rowdy, in a semi-sanctioned fashion. Beyond work, there wasn't much else to do on their cruel little worlds.

Lizzi was in dark maroon mylo—halter top, hot pants, and boots—black hair floating down her back, restrained only by a headband. The team loped along the corridor in long, easy leaps, worries behind them, the night ahead.

A few Holys tried with little success to turn the citizens from their wicked ways. Nearby, a group of bystanders taunted the rose-robed mendicants, a gang by their glowing sigils and writhing tats. Some had bizarre body mods—all in the mix, not the real. But mostly everyone was just out to have a good time.

The *Illawarra* was near the town's marina. The regulars were mostly float pilots, hopping Titan's lakes, but it was also a gathering spot for the sports fans, and they were out in force earlier for the game. By the time the Bombers got there, much of the sports crowd had drifted away, save the die-hards and the drunks.

The message came through Lizzi's comm as they approached the portal. Scattered jeers greeted the half-dozen Beihai players, but most offered friendly congratulations; both teams had played fair and hard. Their captain waved them inside and paused outside.

The words scrolled across her wrist: *Funding not available at this time.* Lizzi clenched her fist.

Let's have a drink. Lizzi growled an incoherent response and flung herself through the portal of the *Illawarra*.

The bar was hot, the walls always projecting the massive, rolling waves of Earth's distant tropical oceans—real oceans, blue oceans, *water* oceans. The projector in the corner had switched to a musical set, two musicians in the real and four more joining in the mix. They were jamming the latest music from down-system, and the mix crowds from three—four?—towns overlapped in the dance space.

She started getting inviting stares as soon as she walked in but ignored them and sauntered towards to the bar.

Nooshin tried to pull Lizzi into the flailing crowd. *Let's dance,* Molly pleaded.

Later, Lizzi signed. Her teammates went off to the dance space, mostly to chat up the locals and maybe connect.

Lizzi grabbed a stool at the bar and signed into the counter left-handed to open a tab. She ordered an ale and a shooter—Bombora (or what passed for it, this far from the grapes of Earth). Distilled from local Titan hydroponic produce, its impact made up for its challenging flavor.

She was feeling moody and torpid, after the ferocity of the game and the frenetic release of sexing in the shower (as sudden as a sneeze—and just about as satisfying). She'd as soon find a sheeple to cuddle and just take a nap. Lizzi drained the ball of vodka and let it sear her throat for a moment, followed by a long, soothing swallow of ale from its sipper. She was halfway through her brew, and oblivion seemed nearer than ever, when Lizzi realized someone was standing too close behind her. Molly turned and they stared back at him.

His comically exaggerated movements in lowgee meant he was from down-system—and well-heeled from the stylish clothes.

"Hi!" Molly said, aloud, startling Lizzi. The hum in her throat, the sound of her own voice coming from *outside* back into her head, always took her by surprise. Lizzi beat *Silence!* on her thigh but Molly ignored her.

The visitor to Titan was surprised as well. "Huh—I mean, pleased to meet you." He licked his lips. "Pardon me, but you caught me by surprise—speaking, I mean."

He was handsome enough, in a carefully modded way, with dark, wavy hair swept back from a prominent brow.

Molly explained, "When we're drinking, the Executive Control system slips just a *teeny* bit…" She raised Lizzi's right hand, waved thumb and forefinger, barely apart, and giggled, leaning back on the bar. "Then we tend to, oh, lose control…"

Molly had absorbed too many romantic immersives; Lizzi hated it when the AI played the man-crazy slut.

Stop.

He stuck out his hand, like some character in an old-time video. "My name's Jude Mathers."

She took it, fingers playing in his palm.

"I'm Molly, by the way—Lizzi's younger, more playful self, you might say. The conversationalist. Pleased to meetcha, stranger."

F.u.g.O.f.f. Lizzi spelled out slowly. She wasn't in the mood for Molly's put-downs—*younger self, prettier self, smarter self…*

Mathers frowned down at the fingers beating on her thigh.

"Lizzi says she's happy to meet you, too—and wants to get to know you better," Molly explained. "Care for a drink?"

"Sure…" He looked around for a menu, then gestured at her bulb of ale. "The same."

She released his hand and tapped the order.

"I watched your game," Mathers said, pulling over a stool and joining her. Lizzi was distressed to feel her body shifting towards his.

"The Bombers are doing well—perhaps a serious shot at reaching the All-System Tourney."

Who? Lizzi signed, and Molly asked, "Are you affiliated with the Roundball League, by any chance?" Her leg closed the gap to his and began stropping slowly. "We can get you autographs if you're a fan." She gestured at the dance floor, where the players, fueled by alcohol or drugs, were writhing through the air. "Anything to improve relations with the League…"

"I'm not with the League, but I could quickly become a fan." They both smiled at his fatuous remark. "Actually, my visit has nothing to do with roundball, per se—but everything to do with you."

Mathers fell silent as the big man behind the bar delivered a pair of stubbies and drink bulbs, and a bowl of crispy critters.

"I'll take the tab," he said to the bartender, waving his wrist over the counter.

The local gave Lizzi a crooked grin, then glanced at the credit line and the tip. He raised an eyebrow.

"Your shout," the bartender drawled in his ANZee accent. He slid away down the bar.

Mathers turned the covered bottle in his hand, amused, and took a sip of ale. He seemed surprised.

"It's an acquired taste," Molly said. "Like many things on Titan." She picked a cricket from the bowl, popped it into her mouth, and munched loudly.

"No; it's not bad." Mathers seemed surprised the ale wasn't worse.

Molly drained one vodka and pointed at the other right-handed, eyebrows raised. When he shook his head, she took it, leaned back, and crushed the bulb, sending a stream from arm's length into her gaping mouth.

He straightened and leaned closer—though a quiet conversation was impossible in the surrounding uproar. *Time for business.* "I represent an Earth-based company interested in your abilities."

"Really?" Molly replied, wide-eyed.

Lizzi waited to see how far the act would take them, hoping the stranger would get to the point quickly. Molly would drink to remain in control—until she lost all control.

Then they'd wake up in a stranger's bed—or worse.

"You're Elizabeth Rio Jin, and you've been inquiring after a visa for Earth—perfectly reasonable, if you make it to Luna for the Tourney—but you haven't been able to get approval. There are certain *impediments* to your travel plans—but perhaps we can help each other."

"We'd be *so* grateful," Molly simpered.

Lizzi took a sip of ale. She didn't like the proximity of this off-worlder, his attempt at gaining their confidence—or Molly's insistent leg.

Standing, Lizzi made a sudden *soubresaut*, rising into the air nearly a meter. As she descended, she grabbed the edge of the counter and perched there neatly.

The bartender frowned at the dark waves floating slowly down behind her.

"Eh! Keep your hair outa my work." Shaking his head, he turned back to the other customers.

Molly rolled her eyes but captured her hair double-handed and drew it over her shoulder to drift into her lap. She proceeded to idly weave her mane into a loose braid, with Lizzi's clumsy help.

"Tell me more," she said, crossing her legs. Her top boot twitched up and down, closer and closer to the off-worlder.

Mathers looked up and continued. "You haven't seen your parents since they…emancipated you, I understand—"

Abandoned. Me. Lizzie signed, the braid forgotten, left hand clenching into a fist.

"—and Earth barred the *haute* augments like you not long after your surgery."

Relax, dear, Molly murmured to Lizzi, stroking her left hand.

Mathers flicked his wrist, delivering a business card to Lizzi's comm. She glanced at her wrist, then back at him, eyes wide.

A.R.X., Liz spelled out, hand thrust into his face. *Did this, you. This*, she repeated, and slapped the U-shaped scar on her head. It drew some curious glances.

"Another drink," Molly said, with some difficulty. "Bandwidth…is dropping." Her crossed leg was twitching in a more agitated fashion. "Can't have that!"

"I'll buy," Mathers replied, "if you'll come down here where we can talk with some privacy."

Molly hopped off the counter, stretched, and returned them to the bar stool. The off-worlder tapped the counter for her, and the bartender appeared with the next round.

The Bombers' captain crushed another bulb of vodka, then sipped her stubby.

She sighed. "Strong emotions can interfere with my executive function," Molly explained.

"ARX has been developing tightly coupled neural

augmentation techniques for decades. The first applications were therapeutic, then more profitable ones. You were a clinical research experiment—the next generation of *homo machina*."

"So you think that, with your help, we could visit downside? See Lizzi's parents?"

"Yes; they're living in SurAm, near your maternal grandparents, in Brasilia."

Her left hand relaxed from a fist, and calmly signed, *Kill them.*

Mathers blinked and stiffened.

You. Understand. Lizzi signed.

He nodded. "I haven't been completely honest with you. Or, I should say, forthcoming. I uploaded IP Sign before I came down here to see you."

"Uploaded?" Molly repeated, leaning closer. "You're an augment too?"

"Yes," he smiled.

"And what did the corporation do for Lizzi's parents?"

"Your—her—parents wanted to return to Earth." Mathers shrugged. "So we helped repatriate them."

"And left Lizzi behind?" Molly pressed.

Mathers shook his head. "It wasn't our intention, or theirs—I think. It's not that they didn't *want* you. But…"

What? Lizzi signed. *Talk.*

"Your parents wanted more children. You know how difficult it is, here. They thought your condition was likely caused by Titan—recycled air, intermittent radiation exposure, vat food—"

"That just sounds like most of Earth," Molly retorted. "Radiation exposure on Titan is unlikely to explain a pediatric tumor. Or the post-surgical stroke that paralyzed her."

Mathers shrugged. "Microgravity then, or the—"

"And the corporation? What about your responsibility?"

"After the stroke, you would have been a paraplegic, mute.

Let's face it: Colonial Medical Services just didn't have the facilities found on Earth, and no one thought you'd survive the drop down the system. So we proposed doing the surgery here, and sponsored it, to give you a better chance."

Then? Lizzi demanded.

"That's the unfortunate part," Mathers admitted. "We didn't expect the politics on Earth would swing so violently. Governments passed the augmentation laws, corporations curtailed development, and the funding vanished. They shut down our Titan lab at Gold Coast. The researchers went back to the inner system. And you were left…here."

Molly asked the question even as it occurred to Lizzi. "What about you—if you're an augment, where do *you* live?"

"In Cleveland, actually—that's on Earth, NorAm. I'm licensed, a loophole in the law." His tone grew confidential again.

"The loopholes were created quietly, out of the public eye. *Quid pro quo.* All the government functions are outsourced to consortia, there, and the consortia wanted Augments to work for them."

"And if we work for you…"

"You can be an exception, too—working for Special Projects."

Play ball, Lizzi signed. *Nothing else matters.*

Molly explained, "Our education was rather limited. Lizzi was training for air ballet, before the illness; then there was the convalescence, the augmentation, a Colonial group home…All we have is roundball."

"Actually Molly—may I call you Molly?—we need you as well as Lizzi. Your combined athletic prowess will open doors for you both. And we may be able to further enhance your capabilities."

"Really?" Her right hand reached out to touch Mather's sleeve, though her left was still clenched at her side.

"We've done some interesting work in the amygdala and nucleus acumbens, since you were activated. Both receptive integration *and* control."

"We could feel emotions, together?"

What job? Lizzi signed.

Mathers glanced down at her hand and answered. "Various tasks… surveillance, false flag ops, near-field signal interception, physical penetration—"

Molly giggled, and Lizzi covered her face with her hand, squeezing her nose hard, trying to concentrate.

She released herself and signed, *Spy.*

"Well, *intelligence analyst*, let's say." Mathers covered her slender right hand in his.

"We'll take care of you," he promised, locking eyes.

Lizzi's left hand came up and removed his, just as their conversation was interrupted.

"*Meimei!* I'm corrupting your little *Sakura*—want to play?"

It was Long Scythe, in a pale clingsuit, with an arm around Cherry and a bulb of something in his other hand. They were flushed and damp-faced from dancing, and the Bomber forward was nuzzling the Whirlwind captain's neck. The pair looked at the downsider with curiosity.

"Or do you already have a date?" Long asked. "Geez, from down the well, but I bet he's got the creds!" The pair laughed.

"We're getting a *room* before it's back to Beihai and cubby-*àiai*," Cherry said. She flattened herself in front of Long, palms up and face turned.

"I…can't…move!" she groaned, sending the pair into a fit of laughter.

"Bombers are catching the redeye float back to Beihai," Molly announced. "*All* of us." She looked pointedly at Cherry.

The AI's restraint surprised Lizzi. For all her silliness, Molly took the team seriously.

"We'll have to make it a quickie, then," Cherry laughed. "Anyway, no *stamina*, him."

"Oh, such claws, my little *Tora*..." Long gave her a hurt look, even as his hand moved down her back and fingertips slipped beneath the waistband of her tights.

"We'll be at the *Crash Pad*," he said, as they walked away. "See you when we see you ... if we see you ..."

He waved over the remaining roundball players, who trailed after Long and Cherry, laughing.

"I don't want to keep you from your friends," Mathers said. "So, to save time, I'll directly upload a contract for you to consider."

Lizzi moved her left hand out of sight. *Raise shields*, she signed to Molly: their code for caution.

He smiled. "We'll match your community fund-raising—or rather, the money will come from a foundation we use—to pay for the entire team's trip. And no visa problems."

He reached out to stroke her cheek. "With a stop for you at Columbia Hills, our facility on Mars, for those upgrades..."

He flicked his wrist at her to upload his contract. The smile faded, as he tried the upload again, and yet again.

Payload contains embedded executable, Molly reported. *It is attempting to open a back door—*

Mathers frowned.

"MLE: unlock, override—" He recited a string of letters and numbers, and looked expectantly at Lizzi.

Don't worry, I've got this, Molly whispered.

Molly smiled, and Lizzi raised her left hand, signing the universally understood middle finger. It took all of their control to stand, however: not the cyber-attack, just too much to drink.

"I..." Mathers cleared his throat. "I meant no disrespect. That was just a test."

Not that drunk, signed Lizzi.

"You should think about your future," Mathers pleaded, "after roundball. What do you have here?"

Friends, Lizzi signed, glaring at him.

He shook his head. "You can be so much more. With enough conditioning, you could even visit Earth. Stand under a blue sky you can breathe—trust me, it's not as bad as they say—not like this, this *tomato bisque* you have here. See a real ocean, the kind you can swim in." He gestured at the scene on the wall, waves washing over Killalea Beach.

Lizzi was having none of it, and Mathers could tell.

"Look—I'll send the contract by comm, then. No tricks. You just demonstrated why you're valuable to us. Just…think about it."

"Hey, killer!" cried Nooshin from down the bar.

"Hi, gorgeous!" said Molly, and moved to join her. "Hey, the evening's young."

Behind her back, Lizzi signed, *We'll see.*

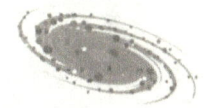

J. L. Royce is an author of science fiction, the macabre, and whatever else strikes him. He lives in the northern reaches of the American Midwest, exploring the wilderness without and within. His work appears in *Allegory, Cosmic Horror Monthly, Fifth Di, Fireside, Ghostlight, Love Letters to Poe, Lovecraftiana, Mysterion, parABnormal, Sci Phi, Strange Aeon, Utopia, Wyldblood,* etc. He is a member of HWA and GLAHW. Some of his anthologized stories may be found at: www.jlroyce.com.

A Limited View

By Gary Kloster

"YOU'RE SIGNING YOUR OWN DEATH WARRANT, PROF," Avi said, staring with disgust at the table between him and his advisor. "Can't you see that?"

"Avi, it's goulash." Professor Lucy Bertoli dug her fork into the steaming red mass that covered her tray. "You should eat some. Low blood sugar makes you dramatic."

"*That* is not goulash," Avi said. "That's a public health emergency. You're going to eat it and die of salmonella and I'll never get my doctorate."

"See what I mean?" Lucy pointed a squirming forkful of noodles at the tablet beside her tray, its screen lit with the latest *Journal of Vertebrate Paleontology*. "What'd you think of Hamilton's article?"

"Courtship displays of the Achillobator?" Avi shoved his untouched lunch aside. "It blows. He recorded what, fifteen seconds of a dromaeosaur hopping in a circle, screeching like a constipated chicken, and from that he deduces a courtship display? Poor thing probably had its foot caught in a hole. That wanker is just fishing for funding."

"Such a smart boy," Lucy said. She had dated Hamilton ages ago, when they were grad students. He *was* a total wanker. And that funding he was after could be going to much more deserving researchers...

Lucy's musings stopped when she spotted a familiar face in the crowded cafeteria, a young woman stalking towards their table, a tray in her hand and a scowl on her face.

"Heads up. Here comes your little ray of sunshine."

Avi barely had time to look up before Gerri dropped into the chair beside him, her own pile of goulash splattering. Dr. Bertoli retrieved her tablet, wiping the red speckles of sauce off its screen while Avi's girlfriend jabbed her fork viciously into her helpless entree.

"I hate this job. I hate physics. I hate time travel. And most of all, I hate researchers. I really, really do." Gerri's bright voice wasn't usually good for menacing growls, but Lucy thought that the tech was pulling it off now.

"Rough morning?" Avi plastered on a sympathetic smile and started to raise an arm to put around Gerri, but then he pulled it back.

Considering the way the young woman was wielding her fork, that seemed like a wise decision to Lucy.

"My morning…" Gerri stared at the dripping noodles impaled on her fork with disgust. "You don't want to hear about."

§

"Well, it can be frustrating."

Lucy frowned at her student, but Avi was looking at Gerri. The boy should just leave it be. Almost time for their viewing, and if Avi got Gerri riled and interfered with that, an annoyed girlfriend would fall way down on his list of worries.

"I mean, if they could just find some way to make this procedure more precise, then you wouldn't have to deal with irate history professors all the time," Avi continued.

"Hey, there's an idea. I'll mention it to Dr. Suke next time I see her. Though I doubt she'll ever leave her lab again, what with all the death threats she's getting from idiotic academics." Gerri's fingers snapped hard across the keys as she entered the settings into the chronoscope. "You researchers have no idea how hard this is. I've got a master's in Physics from Cornell, a year of training, three years of experience, and I'm lucky to hit somewhere within a thousand miles and a hundred years of the target with this thing."

"Which is not your fault, of course," Avi said. "It would just be nice—"

"I *know*, Avi. It would be nice to see the Magna Carta signed. It would be nice to get some popcorn and watch the gladiators. It would be nice to poke around Jerusalem and start fifteen different religious wars. But we can't, okay? Finding a specific event with the chronoscope is like asking a sharpshooter to hit the bullseye of a target that's on a beach when she's riding a speedboat a mile offshore going like hell through a hurricane. It isn't going to happen. Why can't people accept that? I didn't get my degree just so that I could listen to a bunch of liberal arts majors scream about my inability to control temporal physics."

"And you shouldn't have to," Lucy said. "Avi, stop antagonizing your lovely girlfriend and let her finish her preparations." Lucy pointed emphatically to the secondary console beside her. "Practice your species recognition or something, okay?" Her student rolled his eyes, but sat. Lucy turned back to Gerri with her brightest smile. "No worries like that from us, dear. Drop us anywhere in western North America in the late Cretaceous, and we'll be pleased as punch."

Not quite true, since there were plenty of sightings from Lucy's last viewings that she'd love to follow up on, but true enough. The chronoscope had revolutionized paleontology, finally giving researchers like her a chance to study something besides fossilized bone and a few pitiful scraps of surviving organic residue. The advantages of the technology so far outstripped its problems that Lucy felt she had no right to complain.

The historians who were constantly bitching about not being able to focus in on key events would do well to shut up and take what they could get, Lucy thought. Let them try to study Rome using only the bones of its dead for a while. Then they wouldn't complain so much about limits on their data.

"Thank God," Gerri said. "You paleontologists are a blessing. All right, I've got your preferred time and location locked in. Ready?"

"Quite," murmured Lucy as she slipped her hands around the console's controls.

"Here we go then. Activating…now." As usual, nothing happened to signify the event except a *ping* from one of the boxes of equipment hulking beside Gerri.

"Right, initializing. Okay, your viewpoint estimate is somewhere in Montana, about 65 million years ago. I'll work out better numbers soon. You should be getting a picture…now."

The wide screens in front of Avi and Lucy lit up, colored haze slowly resolving into brilliant blue sky, emerald leaves, ochre mud.

"Viewpoint control's yours. Four hours, guys, and the clock's started. Good luck."

Lucy hardly heard Gerri. Only four hours to explore, and she wasn't going to miss a thing. Her hands grabbed the controls, and the forests of the Cretaceous spun around her.

§

The first time Lucy had watched a chronoscope, it had been in an auditorium jammed full of other paleontologists, archaeologists, geologists, and all the other members of the dirty fingernails research crowd. The quickly moving swirl of images across the wide screen had almost made her sick.

She'd forced herself to watch, though, until the images had stabilized. A field being scythed clean by peasants. A mammoth wandering alone through a sea of grass. A mud flat, empty and barren except for a few puddles green with the slime of life. The images and their implications had silenced the room.

Afterward, it hadn't been silent as the questions fell like hail. First, they had to make sure of the impossibility of altering the timeline. After that had come the long argument about the imprecision of the equipment. Lucy, though, had been more interested in how it could be best used.

What she came away with was simple. Any viewing of the past was limited—the window could be held open for only a few hours, and the area that could be seen was only a circle of eight to nine hundred meters radius, centered on the spot where the viewpoint had initialized.

So the swirling motion that had dizzied her in the film was explained: researchers shifting the view as fast as they could, searching for something of interest in the available window to focus on. Speed would be the key to making the most of this technology; speed at moving through the area, spotting the most critical items of interest, and getting the most out of a limited recording time. Lucy realized then that she would need to get over her queasy opinion of rapidly changing perspectives fast.

Luckily, she'd had an immediate idea on that.

On the way home from the presentation she had dropped by her sister's to visit with her nieces and nephews. Then on to the electronics store, to buy a game box and a few of the slickest, fastest first-person shooters the kids could recommend. In six months, she'd gone from a dizzy noob to the third-ranked killer in her age group on her preferred practice ground, *DemonSpore III: The Reckoning*.

Her sister's kids had been mildly impressed.

§

Four hours. Not long enough, not when the waiting period between viewings was measured in months and the pressure to find something interesting to justify the cost of the viewing made

Lucy's palms sweat against the controls.

"Going up," she snapped like a fighter pilot. "Watch our six." The chronoscope presented a perfect, spherical vantage point to the viewer, but it was simpler to divide that view into smaller pieces and have multiple eyes looking it over. Unfortunately, the only viewing theater they could afford was one of the small ones, with just two consoles. That's why she had brought Avi. He had flown drones for the Air Force before college, and he was the only one of Lucy's students that she trusted to keep up with her.

Like a rocket, they spun up out of the trees and their view opened up, a neat circle of the past bounded all around by the dull grey emptiness of nothing. The blankness that surrounded the chronoscope's view area made everything look strangely artificial, like a stage set. It had encouraged a lot of conspiracy theorists to claim that the chronoscope was nothing but a graphics engine fraud.

Lucy barely noticed the empty grey now, though, too focused on searching the land below. Mixed forest and meadow spread beneath her, and water gleamed to one side, the boggy shore of a lake or river whose edge was just visible. Insects hummed through the air and strange cries echoed through the trees. A perfect setting, day and sunny and clear, and Lucy smiled to herself. Then she spotted something.

"In the trees at two o'clock." The branches there shook and danced as small, quick creatures leapt through them.

"More of the proto-squirrels," noted Avi. "Or have they finally decided on a name?"

"No, Percy and Chu are still arguing over who saw them first." Another reason why Lucy only did this with her grad students. She moved the controls, gliding the viewpoint down closer to the scampering creatures.

"Hold it," Avi said.

At her student's voice, Dr. Bertoli's hands froze and her eyes danced across the screens.

"Eight o'clock, close to the edge. I keep getting flickers of motion, something gliding in and out of the view."

"Pteris?"

"Something like. I'm only getting bits of wings and beak. But I think they're circling. Like vultures."

"Take us there." Lucy reluctantly let go, and the image onscreen skewed quickly around as Avi zoomed towards what he'd seen. Lucy watched the forest whip by below, scanning it for other possibilities as they flew over. Dinosaurs seemed preternaturally skilled at stealth and camouflage. Viewings could sometimes feel like a particularly frustrating session of *Where's Waldo?*

Except this Waldo often weighed five tons.

"They were circling right about... Oh holy—"

"What?" Lucy snapped her eyes to the small screen on her console that showed his viewpoint perspective and felt her breath catch. At the edge of the pine forest below, a small stretch of mud and reeds slumped down into brown water. Centered in this clearing lay a body, some kind of hadrosaur. Above the corpse, great jaws working, crouched royalty.

"Oh my Godzilla," Lucy whispered softly. "I think it's the queen herself."

The carnivore was huge, bigger than her prey, and beautiful. Deep green feathers rippled on her back, striped with black like a tiger, a perfect camouflage for the forest's shadows. Her belly gleamed with scales though, a dull gold, and the image of a dragon curled on piles of coins ran through Lucy's mind. Staring silently at the monster, busily hauling out a great red mass of intestines and then leaning back to gulp them down, she felt like she was almost on the verge of tears. One of Lucy's first digs had been a partial of this terrible, beautiful creature.

This was one of her babies.

"A Rex." Avi's voice was tight with excitement.

Lucy's hands somehow stayed steady as she swept the view over the beast, noting the tiny, two-fingered arms, the shape of the head, the body, the huge size... It was so hard to claim certainty when faced with bones clothed in flesh and blood and life, but...

"Oh yes. I do believe so." Avi's whoop startled her, and a ridiculous, frantic part of her wanted to shush him, terrified that he would startle the long-dead creature away from its feeding.

"Calm down. Calm down." That last was partly for herself. No one else had spotted a Rex yet. Besides the thrill of seeing one of her favorites, this footage was going to keep her in funding for the rest of her career.

"We have work to do. We'll need a shot of her dentistry. And I suppose some interior shots of the hadrosaur for anatomy."

"Did you see her eyes?" Avi gasped.

"What?" The threads of organization she had been trying to weave together fell apart and Lucy's hands spun on the controls, trying to see it all.

§

"Fifteen minutes." Gerri's quiet warning sent a shock down Lucy's spine. Time had passed far too fast. They had spent it all watching the Tyrannosaurus feed, glutting herself on the hadrosaur, her golden belly visibly swelling as she reduced her victim to shattered, bloody rags. Lucy was amazed at the sheer amount of meat the beast could pack away, and it had only been a few minutes ago that the Rex had given up and staggered away from her feast to sprawl in the shade of the trees, emerald eyes slipping shut in a gluttonous stupor.

"Okay. I'm going to get a few more close-ups while she's still. Avi, I want you to look back over the remains. I imagine they'll be scavengers starting to move in." He grumbled a little, but Lucy ignored him. Her eyes were tired, her neck stiff, and her hands were pained claws wrapped around the controls, but this had been one of the best afternoons of her life.

"Five minutes." Gerri had left her station once to come see what the excitement was all about, but had turned away from the screens hastily, a little green after watching the queen gulp down a vast mouthful of liver. She'd congratulated them both and hastily gone back to monitoring the equipment. "I'm so glad you guys are happy with that carnage. This sort of thing makes up for the crap I had to put up with this morning."

"And we, my dear, are very, very happy with you today." Lucy smiled at her screen, barely restraining herself from reaching out to pat the great saurian head that glowed on it. "This has been wonderful. I'm going to make sure Avi takes you out for dinner on me at—"

"Control." Avi's voice snapped with command, and Lucy hastily toggled off the override, letting him take the viewpoint.

"What is it?" she asked, staring at the screen as he flicked the view quickly over the ground, away from the sleeping giant, past the corpse into the shadow of the trees.

"Thirty seconds guys," warned Gerri.

"No. No, no, no. Right there… *There!*" Avi stabbed one finger at his screen, and Lucy strained her eyes, barely making out the dim silhouette of something moving beneath the trees.

"What is it?" Then the screens went black as the viewpoint winked out, gone. At his console, Avi began to swear, a long blazing trail of curses that ran the words into one solid expression of frustration.

"What, Avi? What was it?"

He ignored his advisor and stared across at his girlfriend. "Gerri, is there…"

"It's gone, Avi. Gone." Gerri looked both sad and hurt, betrayed by Avi's demand after what for her had been a lovely, peaceful afternoon.

"Avi, what was it?" In response, Avi's fingers danced across his console's keyboard, bringing up the recording of their session. He spun through the hours they had spent watching the queen, and then slowed it down, freezing it in the last few seconds of footage.

"Look."

Dr. Bertoli looked. In the emerald shadows of the trees she could just see it, crouched and staring out into the open, presumably watching the queen as she lay next to her meal. A dinosaur, not very large, bipedal. "It's definitely something new." Exciting to be sure, but finding new dinosaurs was commonplace when using the chronoscope.

"Look," Avi said again. He tapped the console, and the image enlarged and brightened as the computer worked it over.

Definitely a new type. It stood almost upright over its legs, and there was something odd about the articulation of its forelegs. It had a short and stumpy tail, stubby muzzle, and a domed, rounded head. It reminded Lucy of a pachycephalosaur, but not.

"It's something new, Avi. And you found it." Maybe that explained Avi's excitement, though Lucy still didn't think finding a new species could explain why he was so upset about losing sight of it, not after their work today. "You can name it. Maybe."

"I think I'd rather know what they named themselves."

"What?" Lucy stared at him, and in response he tapped the screen. Then she saw it. She'd taken it for a piece of brush before, but pointed out, its shape was obvious. A branch hung from those blunt clawed fingers. Was held, actually, when Lucy acknowledged it, gripped between two fingers on one side and one on the other.

Dr. Bertoli stared at the thumb in shock, then slowly traced that branch down from the hand. At its end she could see a stone, chipped and shaped to form a rough sharp edge and a groove to bind to the branch. An ax, much like the ax Lucy had seen in stone-age anthropology exhibits.

"Oh," she whispered. "Oh, oh, oh."

"What's going on?" Gerri started to walk over from her terminal, but she stopped when Lucy looked up at her.

"Gerri. I'll need the exact time and location stamp of this recording please," Lucy said. "It's essential that we be able to view this area again."

"But Professor—"

"Absolutely essential, Gerri. Absolutely." Trembling on the edge of a discovery that would rock her field, her career, Lucy didn't want to hear Gerri's protests. Her eyes fell back to the screen, staring at the image, so tantalizing, so promising, so vague.

"You're all just alike, aren't you?" Gerri said. "Right. Well, screw it, I'm done." Gerri stalked away, stopping only long enough at the door to glare back at them. "Oh, and Avi, you'll find the stuff that you left in my apartment outside. In the koi pond."

"Gerri?" Avi started, but Lucy cut him off.

"Don't worry about it." Lucy patted her student's shoulder reassuringly. "The recording will have the information we need."

It would, and staring at the screen before her, Lucy knew she would see this scene again. No physicist would deny her that. Or physics itself, for that matter.

"Scroll back. Let's watch it again."

Gary Kloster is a writer, librarian, martial artist, and stay-at-home father. Sometimes all in the same day, but seldom all at the same time. Other stories of his have appeared in *Asimov's*, *Apex*, *Clarkesworld*, *Escape Pod*, and many others. You can find him online at garykloster.com.

Two-Tone

By Elise Stephens

THE FULL MOON WAS A POOR DISTRACTION FROM SEA-SICKNESS, even if it did hold steady in the sky above the infernally rickety ferry deck. Nerr stared again at the white disc hanging brazenly bright in the afternoon sky. If the wedding followed tradition, the full moon meant the ceremony was only one or two days away. The oily smell of the cooking feast made his stomach lurch.

As a last resort, Nerr broke the tube's seal, tipped the scroll free, and unrolled it. He wasn't supposed to peruse his delivery's contents, but he was desperate to avoid losing his stomach. A moment later, his eyes focused, then narrowed.

This scroll was defective. Horribly and unmistakably ruined with splatters of unruly sentiment.

Nerr blinked hard to relinquish the lumastration's images, then studied its calligraphy. The letters were balanced in scale and form, but the indigo and black paint comprised at least three different states—longing, anger, and despair—where a single sentiment should have been applied. And of course, none of these states made appropriate undergirding for the intent of a romantic poem.

His first real job outside of the lumidden, and Nerr was going to deliver a bad product. He felt sorry for his friend Amyr, the lumant who had painted the scroll, but more so Nerr felt annoyed that he'd be blamed for the faulty craftsmanship. In almost all cases, a lumastration's creator was the one to deliver it. Nerr's ineptitude would be implied.

The deck of the Dorac Island ferry rocked loudly beneath him and sea-sickness rose again to intertwine with Nerr's panicked confusion. He doggedly shifted focus onto the scroll's border design.

A rose vine wound through pastoral and garden scenes on all four sides. The vine terminated in a blossoming festoon in the scroll's lower right corner. The petals themselves formed points at their tips, rather than rounded edges.

Nerr studied one of the scenes: a small flock of lambs slept in mountain shadow. The blue ridges were blurred, as if the brushstrokes had been intentionally splayed. These peaks might have been composed of smoke. Nerr shook his head.

Why had Lumanar Hallis approved this? The leader of Nerr's lumidden shouldn't allow such shoddy work to tarnish the school's reputation. And Hallis's own vision of the paint's underlayer would have revealed to him just how off-the-mark this lumastration struck. Someone with normal sight would see a lumastration and sense the sum of all its components as one blended impression. A trained lumant could usually discern three or four of a lumastration's pillar sentiments. But someone who saw the underlayer, a gift that usually manifested in eyes of two different colors, could unwind each nuance down to the thinnest thread, unraveling a lumastration's full meaning.

A new weight sagged on Nerr's shoulders. He was missing something. There had to be a purpose to this delivery that ran deeper than a poorly-made wedding gift.

The sea-sickness won out. Nerr pushed his head over the ferry's guardrail. But instead of clearing his mind, the act of emptying his stomach onto the bumpers only scooped out more room for bewilderment.

§

At the villa of the Chief Justice, Nerr announced himself and was instantly led up a winding tower stair. His eyes stung from the fumes of the bridal dyes even before the servant had ushered him into the chamber. He quickly gathered that the scroll was not for the Chief Justice, after all. It was for his daughter.

"May I present Lady Estil Lavrade, soon to be bride of the renowned Baron Hilf Mogtin. Announcing Nerramin Masson, a lumant from Wessal Lumidden who brings you a delivery."

Nerr stood at the edge of a circular tower room. A giant water lily mosaic dominated the floor and a bed with swan-head posts nestled against the far side. The walls were draped with thick tapestries of sage green, silver, and mulberry threads. Estil had her back to him and faced a white blade of light that cut through the room's sole window. A silk dressing gown hung from her shoulders and her light brown hair was pinned up in curling strips.

Two ceramic dye bowls sat on a low table beside Estil; the traditional midnight blue and bright silver. Blue for the ocean, silver for the mountains.

Estil wriggled her fingers over a bowl as the excess dye dripped free. An attendant was fanning the bride's hands to dry them, then wrapping thin strips of linen over the skin in a tight glove.

"You may go," Estil dismissed her staff, but didn't face Nerr.

When they were alone, Nerr pushed his hood back and was wondering whether he should bow when Estil spun with a flourish, catching him off guard.

Younger than he'd guessed. No more than seventeen. Just a year or two older than he.

"May I see it?" she said softly. Her voice was different, now, higher and more fluid than the one she'd used to direct her servants. She held out her hand for the scroll tube. Though her fingers were clumsy from the hand wrappings, Estil refused his help. She pried out the cork with her teeth, then swept a stack of ironed ribbons off of her vanity table. She unfurled the paper and secured one edge with a brass lantern. As she bent over the scroll, her shoulders stiffened.

"I don't understand," Estil said after only a few seconds' study. "The words are right, but all the lumastrated sentiments are wrong. I thought—" She broke off, pulled a stool from under her bed, and shoved it at Nerr.

Then she gave him an odd look. "You have two-tone eyes," she said. "That's lucky in a lumant, isn't it?"

He nodded.

"Can you see the underlayer?"

He nodded again.

"And did you paint this?" she asked, indicating the scroll.

Dread clutched at him. "No," he said. "The lumant was—"

"Amyr Nifka. Yes, that was to be expected." She motioned for him to sit on the stool. "Look at this." Once he'd settled himself, she said, "Did Amyr tell you about it?"

So she also saw its wrongness. Nerr tilted his head, trying to invoke a new perspective. He mentally lifted the motifs that he'd noted on the ferry ride and spread them out like pottery shards, trying to glimpse the whole vessel. Finally he grasped what had been irking him.

The scroll's crime was not simply a cacophony of sentiments. It was that it had strived clumsily to say just one thing. He bit his tongue. Estil poked his arm impatiently.

"Can you make sense of it?" she demanded. "This lumastration was Amyr's last chance to—" she broke off and a furrow crossed her brow. "Just tell me what you see."

"It's all wrong," Nerr agreed. "Amyr made an opposite pairing between the poem's tone and its partner sentiments."

"Yes, but why?"

Nerr tapped one of the lumastrated roses. "A lumant should always strive to hold one sentiment in steady control while completing a particular color for an object. For example, the lumant holds the concept of 'joy' as he lays down the emerald for this vine. He might return at a later time to edge the leaves with rose-tinted ochre while he carries 'anticipation' in his mind, but all of the vine's emerald hue should embody one consistent tone." Though he'd not yet been allowed to lumastrate without supervision, and thus couldn't properly claim the title *lumant*, Nerr knew this much.

Estil gave a curt nod. "Yes, I know all of that. I learned the preliminaries at Aiken Lumidden, and I can say for certain that no joy was used to color that vine. Fear and regret, maybe."

Nerr balked for a moment. She was good. "Th-that's correct. But you might not see that the gradient of this vine begins with a bittersweet longing at one end and gains greater intensity as it moves inward. It's shifted to despair by the time it reaches here," Nerr's finger hovered over the cluster of roses with strange petals.

Estil's eyes surged to a point on the ceiling. She held them there, then dropped her gaze and crossed her arms. In a strained voice, she said, "Go on."

"The sentiments are wrong," Nerr said, "but all of them follow a spectrum of intensity. It's like a map with paths that swirl and loop, but all reach the same destination."

He moved his hand so she could view the roses without obstruction.

"All roads lead here," Estil murmured. "And the flowers are not even well-done. I studied for less than a year and I could have painted better roses than that."

Nerr grinned.

Estil touched the edge of a red petal. "They resemble tongues of fire more than flowers. Am I imagining this?"

"And the mountains are formed more of smoke than of earth and stone," Nerr said. "There are little clues throughout."

Estil stared at him.

"Amyr wants this burned," Nerr said.

"Burned!" she hissed. "To think I'd destroy this, the last thing he sent…"

"This lumastration has a concealed layer of fire paint," Nerr said, more confidently than he felt.

Fire paint's primary use was the sending of hidden messages. Most fire paint missives were accompanied by burn instructions. Lumastrations were also sometimes painted with streaks of fire paint that glittered under the first rays of firelight, but remained invisible if kept away from flame. This scroll contained neither burn instructions nor evidence of fire paint. The burn message was woven into the images themselves.

Nerr reached for the lantern.

"Not yet." Estil whipped the lumastration off the table and pressed its edge to her lips. Then, with a soundless heave of her chest, she lowered it to the floor and braced it flat with her bare feet. She swallowed, then opened the lantern pane and tipped it onto the floor.

They both sprang back as the paper combusted. The scroll shriveled to small clumps, leaving behind a pale pink luminescence. It was indeed a fire paint note. Nerr breathed silent thanks that his guess had been correct, then held stone-still to watch as glowing letters appeared in spots where illustrations had masked outward traces.

Estil didn't stop him from reading over her shoulder.

What name did you give our child?
May your marriage be a happy one.

-A. N.

Then, in a smaller hand that Nerr recognized as belonging to

Lumanar Hallis:

Help this woman, Nerr. Consider this a test.

A moment more and the fire paint message dimmed to nothing.

After a long silence, Estil spoke hollowly. "Amyr and I met at Aiken Lumidden while he was teaching a landscape series. I was studying there because I was 'too curious and lively' at home. My parents hoped the rigorous academics would keep me in check. Aiken is much more pragmatic about teaching non-lumants than your Wessal. Especially those from wealthy families." She snorted. "But I was expelled when someone discovered I'd gotten myself pregnant during my stay. I assume you can gather the rest."

Before Nerr could reply, Estil said, "Amyr told me about you. Just a few words. He said you shouldered your own burden of injustice and had a heart that might pity our child. You were his choice for the person to trust."

Nerr's neck prickled.

"You have a bloodmark, don't you?" Estil said.

Nerr's mouth had gone dry, but he met her eyes. "The death was an accident. Lira was my friend. My bloodmark, along with the right to lifelong dishonor, was given to me without a fair trial, at least if you ask me and my family. We weren't popular in the town, and there were no witnesses. I said it was an accident, but that wasn't enough for them." Nerr flipped his wrist so Estil could see the lumastrated criminal tattoo. Each time he saw it, he felt the paint's embedded shame, like a lash across his face.

To her credit, Estil didn't cringe.

Nerr said, "I'm only a lumant because my mother thought my two-color eyes meant I'd have the gift for seeing a lumastration's underlayer. With a bloodmark, no one else will apprentice me, did you know that?"

Estil's eyes showed compassion, but all she said was, "Nerramin, I'm forced to seek your help."

Estil raised her bridal-bound hands, palms up. The colors bleeding through the cloth seemed more like wounds than matrimonial symbols. She said, "The scroll we just destroyed was purchased by my betrothed. He'll expect to see the lumastration as proof before delivering the second half of his payment."

"You could send another commission to Wessal in secret."

"There's no time. Hilf will have been informed of today's delivery." Estil turned to her vanity and opened a drawer. Inside lay a row of paint pots, a bundle of brushes, some sponges, and a slender stack of smooth-pressed paper.

"I'd do it myself," she said, "but with these gloves of uselessness, I can't hold a brush. Not to mention that reading Amyr's note has left me dazed and more than a little heartsick."

"You want me to remake the lumastration," Nerr said flatly.

Estil's eyes flashed. "Not just remake. You'll have to do better. The lumastration must convince my future husband." She paused. "You've admitted you see the underlayer. If you think you can deceive me into thinking this task lies beyond your reach, you're wrong." The next moment her jaw softened. "Forgive me. I'm accustomed to having my wishes met with submission. It's done my temper no favors. You were selected by Amyr and the Lumanar of Wessal to deliver this scroll. At least one of them knew it would have to be destroyed in order to read its message."

Nerr nodded. Hallis had told him to help her.

"Which means they also knew you'd be obliged to make a copy."

His throat tightened. That must be the test Hallis had meant. Nerr would paint his first unsupervised lumastration, and it would have to withstand a stranger's scrutiny. There would be no master to observe and offer corrections.

"My lumidden paints have been diluted," Estil said. "It was the only way they'd let me bring them out of Aiken, and even then I used a generous bribe. The effects of the lumastration shouldn't be dimmed by dilution if your technique is good. You have until dawn tomorrow. That is when the gift must be presented to my future husband. Any later and the break in tradition will invite suspicion."

Nerr suddenly remembered something Lumanar Hallis had told him. Nerr had often argued, begged, pleaded to be allowed to use lumidden paints without someone bent over his shoulder, scrutinizing him like a child learning his letters. For an entire year of his apprenticeship Nerr had been refused.

This craft is not made for ambition, Nerramin. It is made for service, Hallis had said. And today Nerr would paint his first lumastration without any official supervision. It was risky, no doubt, but it would help the woman his friend had loved. And Hallis had given him orders.

"I'll do what I can," Nerr said.

§

Nerr stared at the blank sheet and squeezed the brush handle until his fingertips felt paper-thin.

Estil had surrendered her chambers to him for the work, promising pure isolation. He'd swallowed a few bites of something, lit three large lanterns for illumination, and then set up her easel just as the sun slid into its final notch on the canvas of early night.

A shadow flapped across the keyhole window, drawing his eye. In the courtyard below, a pennant rippled skyward, bearing the gold crescent of a shagar lion fang, the Lavrade crest. Beside it flew the blood-red stallion of the Mogtin arms. For a moment, Nerr imagined that the crowd below were not the hired help preparing for a wedding, but soldiers furnishing themselves for the clash of armies. In his imagination, the crests became the war paintings of the Banner Lords, brutal lumastrations used as weapons on the front lines. He shuddered, then rolled his stiff shoulders and turned to his task at hand. He'd less than a day to finish, while an experienced lumant would have devoted three days to such a job. Focus would be essential.

Nerr uncorked a pot of cerulean and one of hunter green. Using the wet palette Estil had prepared for him with a moist sponge and coated paper in a dish, he fed small portions of each color into a base of pure white, adding drops of ochre until he'd achieved a fresh green for the pastoral setting of a love scene. As the brush touched paper, Nerr felt his body glow like a kindled tinderbox.

During his first months at Wessal, Nerr had been steeped in cautioning lectures about the perils of lumidden paints. When at last Nerr had painted with them, he expected to meet pure devastation of body and mind. He'd not once anticipated the joy. Now, as before, Nerr felt his spirit as an ember, flaring with life even as it expired. He felt each throb of his heart as vitality paired with a counterpoint of decay.

Unlike before, he'd have no opportunity to pause for rests. The ache in his bones would quickly consume him, Nerr knew this, but for now the pain enhanced his vision and distilled his senses to their brightest and best.

Nerr refocused on the scroll stretched before him. He'd applied the base layer for field, foliage, and hills without conscious deliberation. The work was sloppily tinged with his own excitement. He laid down his brush and cracked his knuckles in consternation. Every careless personal sentiment that he slipped into this piece would jeopardize its success. He crossed his arms.

Love. Commitment. Desire. Fidelity. These were what a bridal lumastration required. Yet he could claim firsthand experience for none. He had no suitable anchor onto which he might bind his mind. Nerr at last chose a childhood memory: planting seeds with his mother for a vegetable garden. He summoned his hopeful longing for the seeds' first shoots. This wasn't prenuptial anticipation, by any means, but perhaps it was close enough. He cradled his close friendship with his mother, keeping it delicately suspended as he laid strokes of snow onto the mountain peaks and tipped the waves with foam. After a few minutes' work, Nerr whipped his brush away from the paper and bit his cheek. More personal thoughts were springing up, flooding his mental work surface. He paused to release them, hoping to purge his mind.

Why had Hallis forbidden him to lumastrate unsupervised until this moment? Most apprentices gained the lumant title in less than a year, but he'd been held back twice as long. Nerr turned again to the courtyard pennants.

The elderly often grew squeamish in the face of wartime necessities and, while eavesdropping, Nerr had learned that Hallis drew a fearful connection between Nerr's underlayer vision and the Banner Lords' war paintings. Did he truly worry that Nerr would run off to enlist? Hallis was obviously ashamed of a former student who'd done just that. Nerr had also overheard the lumanar confess he was buying time by delaying Nerr's official training, hoping Nerr would develop some kind of wisdom.

But then he'd given Nerr charge of delivering this fire paint scroll and directed him to help Estil, which meant painting its replacement. Did this mean he'd decided Nerr was finally ready to enter the world of lumastration, prepared for the weighty decisions that followed?

Nerr blew out his breath. He'd never finish in time if his thoughts rambled on like this. He flexed his brush arm, then opened a pot of magenta paint and breathed its sharp, peppery fumes. He delved for memories of delight, then noticed fleetingly that most pleasant recollections dated from the days before his bloodmarking. The giddiness of a harvest festival night in which he'd stayed up late to watch stars rain down in streaks. The morning he'd discovered a robin's nest under the roof's eave, then watched in fascination as two eggs hatched into chicks.

Nerr examined his work. The rose petals had flowed from his brush like velvet skirts. They were well-done. He added final touches to the sheep pasture in twilight, the shoreline and waves at dawn, the flower garden at high noon, and the mountains under the stars.

Using a ruler and pencil, Nerr marked text lines, then measured out a standard letter height to maintain scale. He switched his brush to a fine-tip and chose coal-black for the letterwork. A lumastration's wording would draw the most visual scrutiny.

He hesitated. A love poem. What did he possibly know of this? His parents came again to mind. He knew his mother's protective, agonizing love that kept her from sleep when she wept at night for her bloodmarked son's future. He knew his father's stern silence, rooted in concern.

So this is the underlayer. Not just in paints. To dig below the topsoil in all of life and feel the roots below.

Nerr began the letterwork, heart racing. He untangled the layers of his parents' love into unique strands, then overlaid the coal-black foundation with silver as he fixed this second color with his own quavering hope to someday live beyond the crush of criminal guilt. He conjured a future in which he earned a reputation for something good that he'd done, something brave and heroic and worth talking about. He let himself believe there were women of strength and beauty who would not recoil at his bloodmark, but instead seek to hear his story from his own lips before casting their scorn. He envisioned for himself a brilliant career in lumastration, with the proud shadow of Lumanar Hallis beside him as guide.

Hours later, when the paintbrush slipped from his cramping fingers, Nerr's eyes were dry and sticky. His lips stung when he licked them. Far worse than these symptoms, his bones were deeply chilled. Lumastration always brought fire to the bones. A hot bath countered the pain, and frequent rests were prescribed. But to meet Estil's deadline, Nerr had just one relentless way forward. He knew from books he'd read that when the bone-fire turned to ice, it cost the lumant much more.

Nerr swayed and coughed. His body was a frame of wooden rods that had been sanded down to thin wisps, ready to snap. Yet even now, the pain was joined by wild, intrepid joy. Was this the paint's ecstasy, or was it his own heart rejoicing in its victory?

Now I am a true lumant, he thought. *This pain is common to us all. A silent, suffering brotherhood.*

Nerr felt sure he'd one day have the strength to face this ache with greater resilience. But for now, the best thing he could hope for was sleep. Candles flickered in wall sconces. He didn't remember servants entering to light them.

Nerr shuffled to his feet. His second, faltering step failed and he convulsed, narrowly catching himself on the edge of the bed. It was then he heard the gurgle of water from a pitcher's mouth. He watched a servant exit the room, then stared at the ceramic basin in the middle of the chamber. It held a hot bath and shimmered with reflections of gold filigree and inlaid stones.

Nerr had paid the cost and Estil had sent the cure. Nerr dragged himself to the chamber door, bolted it from the inside, and wrestled off his clothes. As he dropped gratefully into the steaming water, he wondered carelessly whether he might fall asleep and drown. A few minutes later, when the ache in his limbs had dimmed to a mild exhaustion, he dried himself with a thick towel, re-dressed, unbolted the door, and stumbled over to the bed.

His cheek pressed against a pillow scented with clover and sandalwood. He fell into it and didn't rise.

§

Nerr woke to the sound of a woman's voice barking commands and tried to fit his tongue back inside his mouth. The voice was the low-pitched tone that Estil used to command obedience.

He sat up, rubbing his eyes. Estil addressed a line of servants carrying various pieces of travel gear: a riding saddle, leather bags, several homespun blankets. They set the equipment into a neat pile, then all but one filed from the room. Estil watched the door close, then turned to Nerr, eyes shining with pleasure.

"My betrothed has seen your lumastration," she told him. "He declares it excellent." She raised her hands in formal gratitude. The bridal wraps were gone. Her flesh was dyed blue-black across her right palm, little finger, and thumb. Her left hand was similarly dyed with burnished silver across the palm and three inner fingers. When the bridal dyes stained in strong colors, it was said to indicate strength of heart.

Estil directed the remaining servant to approach a wall hanging at the room's far end. Nerr watched as Estil and the servant pulled aside the tapestry to reveal a shimmering gilt mirror, taller than Estil by several heads. The servant rolled the mirror aside to display an iron-bound door. Estil pressed her ear to a carved aperture, then thrust a key into the lock. She beckoned Nerr to follow. He obeyed groggily.

Inside, in the space between two large walls, a small room the size of a garden shed was squeezed. Its interior comprised a wooden rocking chair and a narrow lidless chest padded with blankets. A hand-stitched cloth doll sat in the chest's corner with a wooden rattle across its legs. A second door stood ajar, letting streaks of straw-colored light scatter across the floor and mix with the blue hues of Estil's chamber, blending to a jade green.

An elderly servant rocked and shushed a squirming bundle of homespun cloth. Estil took the bundle into her own arms and a tiny hand reached up from the blankets to clutch at Estil's throat. The crying ceased.

"I named her Inya," Estil said softly. "My betrothed, Hilf, can never know my daughter's true identity. Two servants have been trusted with my secret," she glanced at the nursemaid, "and they are loyal to me. If my own father knew the real story, he'd insist my child be sent away and raised in shame, as if she were guilty of some offense. He believes, like the rest of my house, that she's my ward, my brother's surviving child after he and his wife perished in the Fleshburn. You remember the plague's flare in Nestra Valley?"

"Yes. Last summer," Nerr whispered, grogginess now gone. He'd been brought into a guarded secret. This would only end in trouble or debt. Hallis had said to help her. Was there yet more to that task?

Estil said, "You're going to take my daughter away from here. Amyr has found her a good home. She'll live free from a punishing birthright. I will know neither the town nor the family's name or else I'd one day seek her. This is the plan that Amyr and I made: Amyr would send me a final message with the courier he'd chosen to take our child to her new home."

Nerr's head felt like an apple bobbing in a water barrel.

"In return, I'll do everything I can to have your bloodmark removed," Estil said. "My father is the Chief Justice."

She gripped his arm with sudden familiarity. Nerr glanced

down at her blue-stained fingers. The baby squirmed and fussed.

Estil whispered, "Amyr has entrusted you with the fate of those whom he treasures."

Nerr thought of his friend, of the love that would go unfulfilled, of the child who would never know her parents' names. He looked down at the cloth doll.

"I don't know how to take care of babies," he said.

Estil laughed, a bit coldly. "Neither did I."

The nursemaid left to fetch something from the room beyond. Golden light spilled farther into the nursery and Nerr noticed a small lumastration set into a wall niche.

Moon and stars swirled in a blue-violet sky, surrounded by eddies of color. He recognized Estil's soaring joy. She'd centered her love for the child in the heart of the moon, then layered the moonbeams in pale yellow and bone white laced with grief and anger. The sky's warmer tones were dotted with Estil's fantasies of an alternative life spent with the child's father. In the ash gray of the moon's shadow, Estil had placed a vow to bury her tears where even she would not find them.

He gazed at the baby's hand, still fastened to Estil's throat. He'd no way of knowing whether this, too, was part of Hallis' task for him. He only knew that this child had been marked as a bastard before her birth, and though her mark bore no outward sign like his, it would nonetheless yoke her to a stunted future unless something or someone broke her free.

"I'll do it," he said.

§

Every muscle in Nerr's back was inflamed. His "broken arm" lay tucked beneath his cloak in a sling that held the weight of a sleeping baby. He'd stooped and pulled his hood low.

Before he'd left, the nursemaid had dipped her finger in an

herbal tincture and let the baby suck on it, explaining, "She'll sleep deeply for hours now." Nevertheless, Nerr prayed every five steps that the child wouldn't wake.

Estil had given Nerr a sealed letter with a court date that promised an audience with the Chief Justice to request his bloodmark's removal. There was no guarantee of success, but he could never have gained such an audience on his own.

As her final farewell, Estil kissed her daughter three times: once on each eyelid and once on her pink lips. As Nerr left, Estil turned away, ankles pressed together, hands limp, skin a lifeless white as if she'd become the moon from her own painting.

The next moment, Nerr was a fish struggling upstream as he left Dorac Island against the flow of incoming wedding guests. Pipe music darted up through the air, playful and rushed. The rich scent of roasting meat and baking bread hung thickly.

When he'd boarded the ferry to the mainland, Nerr dared to peek at the baby. He brought his hand near her nostrils, felt gentle puffs of breath, and sighed with relief.

A fellow passenger leaned over to gawk. Nerr froze in horror as the woman studied the child's sleeping face. He wanted to shove the woman, crying, "Leave her alone! She's done nothing wrong!" but the woman just smiled and said, "They're prettiest when they're asleep, aren't they?"

Nerr nodded dumbly.

"The small purse will cover your travels," Estil had told him. "The larger one you'll leave with my daughter. Inside your bag is Amyr's letter with the name and town of the family he chose. Don't open it until you've left."

Nerr carried two hefty sacks of provisions for the baby's new home. This explained the line of supplies from earlier. Estil had also surprised him with the gift of her own box of lumidden paints.

"I can always buy more. You've more than earned them,

Lumant Nerr."

Had she known they were his first set of lumidden paints?

On the ferry, Nerr slit the letter's seal. The town wasn't far. He could reach it before nightfall. Once he'd disembarked, he never stopped moving. A fleeting superstition convinced him that as long as he kept moving, the baby would doze. A foul smell from the baby intensified as the day wore on, but he didn't stop to investigate. On an empty street, Nerr caught himself humming a lullaby.

When he at last neared the family's home, he crossed the merchant quarter as business wound down for the day, then climbed a flagstone road up a low hill to a white-and-blue brick arch above the house's door.

He knelt, arms shaking as he slid out of his sling. The sleeping baby turned with lips puckered in hunger as his finger brushed her cheek. Nerr wrapped his cloak around her, then drew a small square of paper from his satchel, praying the baby would lie still for just a moment longer.

Amyr's letter had instructed Nerr to remain anonymous.

There was a tiny pot of fire paint in Estil's collection. Nerr took it out and selected a small calligraphy brush. He crouched on the house's steps and wrote:

Your generosity will grant this child
a chance she couldn't have taken for herself.
Her mother and father thank you.
She too will thank you someday.

He shook the paper dry. As soon as the fire paint had faded, Nerr brushed a swarm of vermilion and violet flames over the words.

§

Nerr's arms had roughened after a long day's ride in the open wind and sun. His cloak remained behind with someone who'd needed it. He envisioned Estil's daughter growing beautiful like her mother, entering a new life unblemished and unmarked, and the thought had kept him warm after sunset. He didn't notice the cold weather's effect on his health until he stood at Wessal's gates and a watery cough seized him. But not even illness could dampen the energy roiling inside him.

Nerr hovered in silent suspension, hand on the bell rope as he paused before announcing his return.

Hallis would be working in his private study just now. Evenings were reserved for the lumanar's own projects. Nerr tilted his head. Hallis must have known of Amyr's love affair, perhaps even known about the child. He'd have recognized the name of the commission's sender, granted the job to Amyr out of compassion, and then allowed Amyr to challenge Nerr with the task of delivering the scroll and painting its replacement.

The entire errand had been a test, Nerr felt sure of it. A test to determine whether Nerr's intuition could be trusted when using lumidden paints. To judge whether Nerr would harm himself to help someone in true need. It had been his lumant examination. His apprenticeship to Hallis might now truly begin in earnest.

Nerr released the bell rope without pulling it. The faint scrape of spoons on bowls in the refectory woke a rumble in his stomach. He chafed the skin on his bare arms, rubbing warmth into them. Wind danced through the gallery arches, crooning softly.

Nerr looked upward to see a pair of early stars swimming above. His life and the life of Estil's child had each found a way forward, into possibility, second chances, and hope. He could not remember a feeling like this: a throbbing silver glow that tinged all it touched with the essence of brighter, stronger color.

He would find a way to paint it.

Elise Stephens' storytelling is influenced by a love for theater and a childhood filled with globetrotting. She's currently writing a novel in the same universe as "Two-Tone" and further glimpses can be found through her short stories "Drowned Prison" (*Galaxy's Edge*, Jan 2021), "Focal Point" (*Haven Spec*, May 2022) and "War Painting" (*Gilded Glass: Twisted Myths and Shattered Fairy Tales*, WordFire Press, July 2022). Her short stories have also appeared in *Analog*, *FIYAH*, *Galaxy's Edge*, *Escape Pod*, and *Writers of the Future Vol 35*. Elise lives with her family in a house with huge windows to supply the vast quantities of light she requires to stay happy. www.EliseStephens.com

Cloudbreaker Above

By Brandon Nolta

GUSTS WHISTLED AND TORE AT CHERNIN as she shifted position within the spiderwork of metal and expansion joints, trying to stay comfortable for a few minutes more. The last news she'd heard before leaving the ugliest building in the Erewhon said a storm was due around 8 p.m., and Chernin wanted to be hidden aboard the *Cloudbreaker* before the docking crew buttoned it up to fly across the ocean.

Steps from the rubber-coated platform overhead shook her perch, and Chernin froze. No docker would climb down among the support beams and shift absorbers to pull her into the coppers' cold embrace, but they could report her, have the blue and burly law waiting at every balcony and window in Empire Point. She'd have to come out eventually, but she only intended to go up. The trick was to avoid the crew.

Chernin breathed through her mouth, waiting for the voices above to go inside. A cigarette butt spun over the top rail, and with a laugh, the voices headed away from the gangplank. On a calmer day, Chernin knew she could wait for the heavy thrum of the double doors closing, but with the rising wind in her ears, she could miss the sound and lose her chance.

The steps faded from hearing, and Chernin took a deep breath. Best to be quick, she knew, and began her climb to the platform. Too soon, she reached the platform's edge. Now that she was almost there, fear coiled inside her. What if she slipped? What if they caught her and threw her in a hole for daring to climb so close? What if she never saw the *Cloudbreaker* rise again?

"Idiot," she muttered, and cautiously lifted her head past the platform. Her heart sped up, and for a moment, the shadows from the docking lights and the iron sky looked like a knot of sailors, ready to grab her. She imagined how she would look to them: pale skin, shadow-black hair, eyes wide and childish, even though she was days past her 15th year. Old enough to sign onto Aerofleet, were she from one of the right families, or any family. But the light shifted, and there was nobody there.

Quickly, she scrambled onto the platform and crouched at the gangplank's foot, scanning past its rubber-coated metal length for crew at the entryway or shadows just inside. Her luck continued to hold. Clutching the canvas knapsack that held everything she owned, Chernin skittered up the gangplank into the *Cloudbreaker*'s starboard compartment.

From memory, she counted off the turns and passages she'd memorized from the plans in the City Archives until she found a small nook that would be safe from inspection for a while. To reach the entrance, she had to climb over storage crates, which should be too much work for most crew.

Chernin sat back against the warm control bank and let out a long whispering sigh. She wouldn't be completely safe until the *Cloudbreaker* was underway, but getting on board was half the struggle, she thought. Dodging the crew would be tough once they left port, but Chernin had studied everything she could find about the *Cloudbreaker*. If anyone besides its builders knew this bauble of brass and chrome, she did. She could stay hidden, a mouse in the machinery, as long as needed.

Smiling at the image of herself with mouse ears and whiskers, running along the pipes and passages of the great ship, Chernin fell asleep, exhaustion and fear fading in the warmth and hum of the airship's pre-flight activity.

§

Chernin first thought a pocket of turbulence woke her, a moment of shaking that arrived and passed before her mind caught up. Her eyes opened to off-shift dimness, standard illumination on the night watch according to every manual and wireless program she'd ever devoured, and she listened for crewpeople moving about. All she heard was the hum of machinery and the click of switches.

Surely there's at least one insomniac on watch, Chernin thought as she stretched, yawning. Moving slowly, she stood and listened intently. Nobody walked by. No voices echoed down the hall, or sounds of bored card games, or whatever the crew did while waiting out the night. Chernin frowned. Years of stories from any crewfolk she found taught that ships were never completely silent.

There was no help for it; she'd have to look. As quietly and quickly as she dared, she balanced herself on a crate and leaned out, strong arms holding her upper body up. Her head barely cleared the crate's front edge, but it was enough. She glanced down the passage to her right, whipped her head left, and pulled back out of sight. Nothing and no one could be seen in either direction.

A bolt of fear rushed through her. Had they even left? Maybe the storm had passed, and the *Cloudbreaker* was still moored to Empire Point, waiting until they found the little Chernin in the walls. Chernin turned, breathing as silently as her burning lungs could manage. Nobody behind her, no shadows edging near. She listened, ears straining.

Nothing.

The cabin bumped. Chernin braced herself against the crate. Was that what flying felt like? She planted her feet wide and waited, trying to get a feel for the cabin's motion. Chernin felt the floor drop a touch, sensed the cabin swoop slightly starboard. She smiled. If the *Cloudbreaker* was still moored, it was a loose job. The vibrations and balance shifts said she was in flight.

One way to be sure, Chernin thought. There was a porthole two compartments toward the bow from her hiding place. Actually, there were two, one on each side of the cabin. The porthole closest to her was by a crew station, but the portside one was in a hallway. That would be better, Chernin knew, but she'd have to cross the width of the cabin. *No point in daring the crew to find me*, she decided. As silently as she could, she crawled over the concealing crates and stepped into the lengthwise passage. She looked both ways and saw no one.

Five breathless steps later, she was in the crosswise connector, steeped in darkness through the center and lit at either end from the lengthwise passages. Chernin worked her way across, back to the wall, breathing in shaky inhales. At the portside passage, she darted her head around the corner. Nobody toward the stern, and with a sideways motion that hurt her head, she looked toward the bow. Nobody there, either.

Maybe I was wrong, Chernin thought, and decided she might as well risk the look outside. She took a deep breath, strode across the passage, and put her face to clear cold glass encircled in riveted metal. Outside, inchoate darkness surrounded the *Cloudbreaker*. Chernin cupped her hands against her temples to block out the light. For a moment, the darkness refused to clear, until a cloud shifted to reveal a brilliant half-moon. The night sky resolved into a broken cloud layer above patches of glimmering water and darkened land speckled with lights, over which the *Cloudbreaker* now sailed.

Chernin smiled, her reflected grin a dash of bright against the black. Her plan worked. An Erewhon orphan was in flight aboard Aerofleet's greatest ship, and nobody knew but her. *For now, anyway*, the thought came, and her delight vanished as she pulled away and scanned her surroundings, straining to catch any movement of the crew. She darted into the relative shadows of the connector and willed herself not to run back to her hiding space.

Surely the crew isn't all asleep, Chernin thought. *Maybe they don't bustle around much, but there must be some movement. I need to know where they are, and how many. No time is better than now.*

The words, oft said by her nearly forgotten father, didn't comfort her, but she knew their truth. In flight, the *Cloudbreaker* would never sleep more soundly than now. If Chernin wanted to explore, caution demanded she begin. She slowly peeked out into the portside hallway, turned to face the stern, and crept quietly along its length, breath too fast and loud in her ears with each step.

Chernin paused at every door and entry to check for shadows and whispers, and peered around each jamb and corner, searching for crew. By the time Chernin reached the galley, she was puzzled, but as she reached the engine room, with its rows of generators and turbines and capacitors, foreboding joined her confusion. Every room, every space aboard the *Cloudbreaker* save for where she stood was empty, as if it had never taken flight.

The urge to recheck the closest porthole seized her, but she forced herself to enter the engine room instead. Banks of machines, tubes, and gears and devices for which she had no name or purpose surrounded her. Humming, low and soothing, buzzed against her skin, and the heat of machinery and circuits cocooned her. Chernin knew she was at great risk here—a platoon of dancing mechanics could be here and she wouldn't know—but this was the *Cloudbreaker*'s heart. It could never be unoccupied.

But it was. After long minutes of patient, then frantic, searching of every passage and cubby, Chernin knew no one was manning the engine room. The single most important place aboard, and—

Not true, she realized. There was one other place to look. Maybe the *Cloudbreaker* could fly with an empty heart, but not an empty brain. No ship could fly without a pilot, a captain. The bridge was where she had to go.

Chernin took a deep breath, inhaling vapors of mineral oil and ozone, and turned for the bow. This time, she would walk the starboard corridor, carefully but not hiding, hoping to find someone, anyone. Cautiously, Chernin began the long walk forward. Facts, measurements, irrelevant information surged through her as she passed darkened doorways to empty rooms, the moonlit outside no longer as lovely. Each step echoed as she walked, past the crew quarters, the galley, a crew head, then another. Relays clicked, the *Cloudbreaker* hummed, but Chernin heard only her own noises.

After unending minutes, she reached the *Cloudbreaker*'s bridge, marked by an oaken door riveted with brass and copper, and an inset window rimmed in chrome just a few centimeters beyond where tiptoes could take her. Chernin put her hand on the heavy lever and listened. The brass was cool, almost cold on her skin. She heard, felt nothing.

Her father's words echoing in her thoughts, Chernin turned the handle and pushed. The door opened, revealing a fully functioning, clean bridge, decked out in the Aerofleet's finest decorations, and totally, unmistakably empty. Wherever she sailed aboard the *Cloudbreaker*, she was going there alone.

§

Dawn flooded the horizon, gold and pink against the empty blue sea below. Chernin had never seen such an explosion of color; by the time morning light reached the Erewhon, it was stained by soot and shadow. Terror had receded enough that she could marvel at the moment.

Her stomach growled, a hungry rumble in the silence. She'd retrieved her knapsack before falling asleep in the captain's great swiveling chair, and she inventoried her food stores quickly: a couple of apples, half a loaf of bread, and a chunk of waxy cheese. Not the best breakfast, but enough.

While she chewed a hard yellow apple better suited for throwing, she considered her next steps. She had no idea where the *Cloudbreaker* was headed, or how long the flight was. Her plans had been based around avoiding the crew, but while that problem was seemingly solved, she had different ones to consider. How was the *Cloudbreaker* flying without a crew? Chernin thought answering this question might take care of others.

Climbing from the captain's chair, Chernin took a closer look at the stations arranged in a half-moon around her. Clean and chrome, they glistened in the brilliant morning as if the crew had just finished cleaning detail. Chernin had seen pictures and schematics, but never had the chance to examine them personally. She approached them slowly, careful not to touch them and leave some imperfection. Her eyes scanned the controls, listing every function and measurement she'd come to know from the libraries and the City Archive, until she came to one she didn't know: AUTOMATIC NAVIGATION SYSTEM. The light below the label was steady green in mute concert with the others, but no other information was forthcoming.

Chernin read the unfamiliar term again and again, puzzling over its meaning. She'd read of engineering systems described as automatic, but those were simple feedback loops, mechanisms that didn't require human oversight. Chernin froze in mid-thought. Automatic navigation: could that mean the *Cloudbreaker* itself was determining its course, or already had one? Since no one else was aboard, Chernin decided that must be the case. She turned to the pilot's command station on her right. If that was the case, perhaps another such system was here, Chernin thought.

And there it was, below the velocity gauge: AUTOMATIC PILOT SYSTEM. Bright green, like the other, and steady as the *Cloudbreaker* hummed. Chernin realized there was no trick, no mistake. She'd stowed away aboard an empty ship, almost certainly the first Aerofleet ship to fly itself uncrewed, maybe the only ship that could. No captain, no crew, one passenger.

All that effort, Chernin thought, *and I sneak aboard the only ship I didn't have to*. Her laughter echoed around the immaculate bridge, bounding off metal and wood. Outside, the morning grew in strength, warm over the ocean's watery expanse, and Chernin smiled as her laughing subsided. One constant from every conversation and complaint she'd ever eavesdropped on was that management was always ready to take shortcuts with crew wages, with a ready library of excuses to reduce bonuses or dock pay. A crewless boat would be Aerofleet's golden grail, then. No crew to pay, more room for freight because no crew quarters or—

Chernin's eyes went wide.

Or a galley.

Heart racing, Chernin bolted to her feet and ran for the door. Even as reason told her to remain calm, she rushed down the hallway to the galley, to the crew quarters, to the officers' lounge, any room that might hold supplies. After that, she gave up logic, and searched everywhere that might hold anything.

Noon came and went before a trembling, exhausted Chernin sat outside the engine room and admitted that other than what she'd brought, there was no food or water aboard the *Cloudbreaker* at all. The galley's shelves were bare, the freight storage areas empty. Even the plumbing had been drained. If Aerofleet were out to discourage stowaways, they'd found a sure method, she thought.

Slowly, Chernin calmed down. *Try and think yourself out of trouble*, she told herself. If nothing else, she was safe from discovery. Her search of the *Cloudbreaker* was thorough; she was undoubtedly alone. Little food and no water was the obvious problem. *Either I need to find it*, she thought, *or hold on until the* Cloudbreaker *docks. When is that?*

Captain's log, Chernin thought. She'd found it earlier behind a stout but empty jug from England, but hadn't stopped to read it. With forced calm, Chernin stood and walked toward the captain's cabin, near the bow. Soon, she had the leather-bound journal in hand and was leafing through the pages, searching for information about the *Cloudbreaker*'s solo journey.

§

1902 14 May

Refit at Empire Point underway in preparation for maiden uncrewed flight. Tests with four-man Aerofleet scout Nike *very successful, so* Cloudbreaker *chosen for first flight with complete automatic systems, despite my objections to setting sail with no onboard backup crew. High Command believes reliance on automatic systems with auxiliary Marconi wireless flight control will make for better press. Further objection on my part, it has been made clear, will meet with reprisal. So be it.*

Nicholas Hardiman, captain

1902 15 May

Dockside tests of automatic systems complete, with results green across the board. My own misgivings aside, Cloudbreaker *continues to perform admirably as always. High Command has decreed the uncrewed shakedown cruise will be flown on an empty hull, so all normal amenities—food, water, crew accommodations, even the soap and flush tanks for the head—are to be emptied or removed. Once the draining is complete and the weather calms,* Cloudbreaker *will be launched, and my crew and I begin our*

*mandatory leave. Six paid weeks off; the prospect of an automatic
Aerofleet has High Command feeling generous.*

   Nicholas Hardiman, captain

§

Chernin flipped through the remaining pages rapidly, hoping
to stop the leaden dread coiling inside her, but Hardiman's entry
on May 15th, five days prior, was the last. Six weeks in flight; with
no food or water, she wouldn't make it to dock. She would die
alone, a footnote in Aerofleet history, and the *Cloudbreaker* would
be her tomb. Chernin felt fear clawing up her throat and clenched
her jaws tight.

I will not panic, she thought.

She stood, and felt the floor lurch a fraction to starboard. The
light from the passageway dimmed to a shadowy hue. The floor
lurched again. A gentle sound, sizzling in the quiet, rose from the
passageway. Chernin blinked, and slowly, the realization stole
through her: rain.

She turned to the cupboard where she'd found the captain's
log, still open. The empty jug sat there, and Chernin smiled. *Too
early to ready my funeral*, she thought, and grabbed the heavy
glass container from the cupboard. An old smell of peat and hops
wafted out when she removed the cork. Her nose wrinkled, but the
jug was dry. She walked back to the bridge, jug cradled in her
arms.

After taking a too-small bite of hard cheese—*ration for now*,
she thought, gazing longingly at the remainder as she returned it—
she walked along the forward windows until she found a manual
latch on the port side. Gray clouds massed along the horizon, and
Chernin smelled moisture on the wind as she opened the window.
A sharp breeze blew past her as she considered how to capture the
rain. The ledge was too narrow to safely set the jug on, and holding

it outside the cabin was dangerous. Plus, the jug's mouth was too narrow to let much water in quickly.

A patter of drops struck her, spattering her with cold. Brisk wetness soaked the sleeve of her shirt, and an answer presented itself. Rummaging through her bag, she found a clean, thin cotton shirt. She tied one sleeve to the window latch, hung the shirt outside, and closed the window as the gunmetal heavens opened and poured cold rain. Her shirt was soon soaked heavy, and she pulled it in and carefully squeezed water into the jug. With the window open and the jug uncorked, she retied the shirt to the latch and repeated the process again and again as rain pounded the *Cloudbreaker*.

Nearly fifty minutes passed before the last raindrop fell and Chernin recorked the jug. She hefted the water-slicked bottle; about three-quarters full. Thirst sated from the rain, Chernin grinned at the evening sky and closed the window. *If only manna would fall*, she thought as she sat in the captain's chair, calculating how much she could safely eat.

§

Chernin found sleeping more difficult that night, even after the success of nearly filling the captain's jug. Dreams of starvation and skeletons haunted her until just before dawn, when she startled awake in the slowly strengthening day. Chernin settled back in the chair, letting her heart slow to normal as she contemplated the days ahead. Fortune had favored her with rain, but she wouldn't have such luck with food.

Chernin stood up and began pacing, rubbing sleep from her eyes while she thought. Having searched the *Cloudbreaker* up and down, she knew there were no tools aboard, so taking over or disabling the automatic systems was out of the question. Manual controls were turned off; before falling asleep, she'd spun the tiller, flipped switches, and attempted to alter engine speed and revolutions to no avail. No tools meant she couldn't access or use the emergency valves, so shutting down the engines or releasing the hydrogen that kept the *Cloudbreaker* aloft was out. Chernin couldn't even access the wireless, as the microphone and tuner didn't work.

So, Chernin thought, *how can I survive? There aren't any supplies aboard—the storage crates are filled with sawdust and ballast—and even if I stretch the jug's contents or refill it, can I make my food last? Can I get more somehow?*

Chernin turned to look out the nearest starboard window. Far below, a forested mountain range sat, sprinkled with snow and the occasional settlement. There were no maps onboard and nothing to indicate whether she was over Oregon or Oz. As she gazed over the wilderness, she saw a flock of white birds, arrowing through the sky below to somewhere else. *If only I could catch one*, she thought. *Catch, kill, and prepare one*, she amended, and shuddered at the thought.

For a moment, she considered what it might be like to cut short starvation by climbing through the window and letting herself fall. The gnawing in her belly was barely slowed by the small portion she restricted herself to daily, and when that ran out, the pains would only grow worse as her body ground to a stop, dying by inches. Starvation wasn't uncommon in the Erewhon, and it was always ugly.

Chernin sighed and forced the idea aside. She still had time, and hope. *I've repeatedly reviewed all my options*, she thought, *but if I can move and think, there's still some chance of salvation. Gravity will still be there when I'm out of time.*

Chance and hope, she thought. On the far horizon, the sun began its downward trek, and Chernin prepared her evening mouthful of food.

§

A cold breeze from the open window woke Chernin to a chilly blackness, only the stars and the internal dials lighting the bridge. She stretched, stood to get the blood flowing again. Below the *Cloudbreaker*, an ocean of darkness lay upon the world, broken only by the pale glimmering of snow or the liquid shine of water. *I could almost be sailing instead of flying*, she thought. *Surely the dark is as deep as the ocean.*

"A great flying boat," Chernin said aloud as she closed the window, and a memory shifted, a recollection of reading about the crashes and mishaps Aerofleet suffered in the early years, immediately after the War Between the States, before Reconstruction and powered airships made the South a rich tourist hub. Aerofleet lost entire crews to Caribbean weather and cold Atlantic storms, and installed numerous safety features aboard their airships in response. With the dawn of passenger airship travel, those features became standard, including lifeboats.

A burst of hope flowed through Chernin, warming her. *If Aerofleet lifeboats are anything like the naval kind,* she thought, *there might be supplies on them. If there's a lifeboat, if I can get to it, if there are supplies...so many ifs*, Chernin thought, but the chance was enough for now. There were bunks in the crew quarters, but somehow Chernin felt safest in the captain's chair, among the empty bridge stations and controls. Sleep stole over her, hopeful again.

§

Hunger woke Chernin just after dawn, the morning sun already vanished into grey overcast. *A dreary day*, she thought, *but not rainy or windy; lucky there*. Chernin doubted she'd be able to access any lifeboats from the main cabin, which left her less-desirable options. Best bet would be astern, past the engine room and its works, but she couldn't recall if the *Cloudbreaker* had any. Whether that was hunger or lack of information, she didn't know.

After a sip of water and the last bite of a heavily browned apple, Chernin squared her shoulders and walked toward the stern, heart pounding. Despite her excitement from the night before, every step felt like pushing through syrup, and her stomach—already afire with hunger—knotted into smaller and smaller compressions. She'd been all throughout the ship, short of climbing inside the envelope that kept them aloft. Could she have missed a lifeboat?

"I wasn't looking for one before," Chernin said aloud, and kept walking. She would know soon enough. She took a deep breath at the heavy engine room door, then opened it and walked in. Engine room lighting was always on, so the dim glow from the overheads didn't waver or fade as she entered. Between the eternal hum and buzz of the machines and the smell of lubricants and machined metal, Chernin knew she wouldn't be able to stay long without getting ill, so she hurried through the narrow spaces and rows quickly. Against the rear bulkhead of the cabin on the port side, she found a recessed hatch with the legend LIFEBOAT ACCESS stenciled in black. *I hope Aerofleet left them in place*, Chernin thought, and grasped the handle.

With a shuddering bang, the hatch flew open, and Chernin let go of the handle as she instinctively flinched. A neat grey square of sky beamed through the opening, wafting in cold air. In the distance, a hawk soared among the clouds. A black rubber-coated walkway with holes burred through stretched toward the massive rudder hanging at the far end of the *Cloudbreaker*, a movable cross steering a metal cocoon. Thin rails ran at knee and handrail height the length of the walkway, and turned left 90 degrees to box in a bowed railing arching down from the top of the cabin.

Chernin grasped the edge of the hatchway and pulled herself partway through. A soft breeze ruffled her hair, and she inhaled deeply, driving the engine room's funk from her lungs. She looked down, and a rush of dizziness flowed up her. Such altitude, and nothing but empty air below...

She closed her eyes tightly against rising panic. The world tilted, and she forced her breathing into a deep, regular pattern, ignoring the suffocation squeezing her. Minutes passed, and her heart gradually resumed a softer pace. She opened her eyes slowly, letting her eyes acclimate. The *Cloudbreaker* still soared, but her head was clear, and she focused on the walkway and solid construction around her.

Carefully, Chernin pulled herself completely through the hatchway and grasped the handrail on her left. She unfolded herself onto the walkway and stood upright, both hands firmly gripping a handrail. Breezes skirled around her as she stepped forward, then again. Making the left turn at the bend took some doing, but she managed it. *Wouldn't father be proud*, Chernin thought.

The lifeboat cradle sat at the cabin's midpoint, and Chernin was relieved to see that Aerofleet's scouring of the *Cloudbreaker* did not extend to lifeboats. There were two, stacked vertically and covered with stout canvas skirts fitted tightly to pegs spaced evenly along the gunwales. Below the keel of the lowest lifeboat was a metal frame with hinges to keep the lifeboats from falling out. *Glad that's there*, Chernin thought as she pondered how to climb into the lifeboat. Dropping the lifeboat down would make it easier to enter, but she didn't want to risk an accidental drop.

So, I'll climb, Chernin thought. The gunwale of the lowest lifeboat was almost even with the rail at her knees. By climbing over the handrail, she could almost step directly into the boat, once the canvas was unfastened. There was a gate that would simplify matters, but it had been locked for the shakedown cruise. She squatted and reached through the handrails; the canvas was firm, but the fasteners were made to be undone quickly, and she soon figured it out. Chernin quickly uncovered most of the nearest side, and then it was time to do the part she feared.

Quickly, before her nerve failed, Chernin grabbed the arched railing and levered her leg over the handrail, straddling the top rail as she stretched out her left foot to catch the lifeboat's gunwale. The *Cloudbreaker* rocked gently, and she caught herself on the lifeboat. She leaned out into the clear air and found purchase on a seat in the lifeboat. With a soft grunt, she swung her right leg up and onto the railing. Pushing against it, she stepped into the lifeboat and sat down, her grip sliding down the track without loosening. The lifeboat rocked lightly on its gimbals, and Chernin scooted toward the center, pushing against the canvas.

Once she got used to the slight rocking, and her heart beat at a slower pace, Chernin began to search the boat for supplies. They didn't take long to find. A compartment under the bow seat was clearly marked EMERGENCY SUPPLIES, and Chernin almost skinned her knees racing toward it. Trembling, she reached for the handle and gently opened the door. Reaching in, she pulled out expected items: flares, life jackets, a tightly stoppered metal canister of water, a waterproof journal with pencil for keeping navigation notes. Finally, Chernin found a series of steel cans with simple labels. Beef, peaches, potatoes: simple food, but food all the same. A burst of joy bloomed inside her.

Putting the food aside, Chernin continued to empty the compartment until there was nothing more. She began to inventory what she had, carefully noting everything in the journal. As the inventory lengthened, Chernin felt a frown grow. She reviewed her list, then every item again. By the third review, her frown had drawn into a grimace, her earlier excitement sunk into dread. For whatever reason—neglect, error, a prank—the supplies didn't include a can opener.

Chernin looked at the items arrayed around her, then at the blank sky beyond the *Cloudbreaker*. Tears pooled in her eyes as she felt a laugh fighting its way up her throat. *It's funny*, she thought. *Surrounded by food I can't eat, stowed away on a ship with no crew. When they find me, I'll be a withered heap surrounded by plenty. Won't they laugh then?*

Thoughts skittered and flashed across Chernin's mind, and for a long, painful moment, panic clawed its way through her. She closed her eyes and tilted her head back until she faced upward, as if looking up at the Milky Way. A deep breath, then exhale. Again. Once more. Chernin waited until she felt like herself again, then opened her eyes. She twisted carefully in her seat until she could see the length of the lifeboat, looking at the empty space under the stern seat, then turned her gaze back to the other lifeboat. White planking, reassuring in its solidity, hung above her. The metal framework around the arched railing was not as solid as she would like, but there were footholds and supports to grip. If she were well-fed, and not thousands of feet high, climbing would be simple.

Chernin reached out and grabbed a support branching off the starboard arched railing, moving before resolve or energy could fail. Reaching, grasping, lifting herself up with as much care and direction as she had, she pulled herself up the metalwork until she was slightly above and to the right of the second lifeboat, suspended below the cabin's roof. As quickly as she dared, she released the fasteners along the side and peak of the gunwales and threw the canvas back. Chernin braced herself, and as she swung her leg over the gunwale, the *Cloudbreaker* bumped as if running over a broken cobblestone. Chernin gasped and hugged a horizontal beam as her foot dropped and slipped inside the lifeboat.

She held her breath, waiting for another bump. The *Cloudbreaker* flew on smoothly, and Chernin slowly unclenched her aching muscles.

Keeping her right arm hooked around the beam, Chernin reached out and grasped the gunwale, wrapping her fingers around the thick recessed lip. She knew that if she thought too long, she would lose her nerve and then her grip, so she half-pulled, half-shoved her body into the boat, hoping that a last-moment swivel of the gimbals wouldn't cast her to the earth. Chernin felt suspended for a long second, caught between the sky and gravity's embrace.

Then she felt the scrape of strong wood along her side and knees, and even as the boat swung side to side, Chernin knew she'd succeeded. Lifting her head, she saw that she was facing the stern and its empty area beneath the seat, so she turned around, crawling along the keel until she faced EMERGENCY SUPPLIES once again. All she could hear was the thunder of waves, thrumming in her ears as air whistled in her lungs.

"No time is better than now," Chernin said and, with sure fingers and a jolt of wild hope in her heart, she opened the compartment door.

§

Nicholas Hardiman stood at the mooring dock atop Empire Point, watching the shape of his future change as the *Cloudbreaker* gently pulled alongside, settling into the locks as the Aerofleet crew tied the great airship to its berth. He raised his hand and signaled to the chief moorsman as he descended the spidery steps to the gangplank. Unlike many captains, he respected the dockside branch of Aerofleet and made a point not to interfere with their work, but a captain always had to board first. To Hardiman, that was immutable natural law.

The chief moorsman undid the hatch and lowered the steps,

stepping aside smoothly as he did. Most dockside crews complied with captains' quirks, but Hardiman was liked and respected among the crews, and for him, their obedience was unforced and honest. Hardiman flashed a crisp salute as he approached, returning the chief moorsman's gesture precisely.

"Thanks, chief," Hardiman said as he mounted the steps.

The chief nodded and started to reply, but Hardiman stopped abruptly on the top step, his back foot still planted on the next-lowest level. He leaned forward, sniffing the air. His hands tightened at the hatchway's sides, and the chief saw the captain's shoulders tense. Hardiman looked slowly around the inside of the cabin, peering at every inch.

"Chief," Hardiman said.

"Sir?" the chief replied.

"Step up here a moment, please," Hardiman leaned to the side, one hand casually gripping the entryway. The chief bounded up the steps and met Hardiman's gaze at the top.

"Take a whiff," Hardiman said, gesturing at the *Cloudbreaker*'s interior.

The chief frowned, but the captain's meaning was clear, so he leaned forward and inhaled deeply. To his surprise, there was a smell, insubstantial but there. More surprisingly, it was a familiar odor. The chief had a full house of children, in-laws, and his wife, and it took only a moment to place it.

"Somebody hasn't bathed in a while," the chief said.

"Indeed not," Hardiman agreed. "But this flight was unmanned."

The chief gestured sharply at the ground crew, pointing at the cargo hold as the crew assembled. "Wasn't this a six-week flight, sir? There were no provisions on board, so…"

Hardiman nodded. "The smell might have been worse recently. Let's search, but carefully."

They climbed down the steps and met the crew at the cargo hold entrance, outlining their suspicions and instructions in quick, terse statements. With practiced movements, the crew undogged the cargo hatch, swung it open, and boarded the *Cloudbreaker*, their minds on what they might find. A cursory search found nothing, as did the more detailed search Hardiman personally supervised. If the *Cloudbreaker* had flown with a stowaway of any kind, whoever it was made themselves scarce before Hardiman could discover them, leaving only the familiar olfactory evidence of effort and sweat without recourse to bathing.

Twilight found Hardiman standing alone on *Cloudbreaker*'s bridge, gazing over the skyline beyond Empire Point, a maze of steel and glass and airship masts. Whoever the stowaway had been, there was no way to know; every trace had been cleared away. A diligent steward might see an incomplete cleaning, a hurried polish, but no information beyond that. Despite this, Hardiman remained unsettled. Someone had violated his ship. The fact that whoever it was had cleaned up after themselves was irrelevant.

Still, Hardiman admitted as the daylight turned to molten gold around him, there was nothing he could do currently. He would have to search again tomorrow, perhaps with the metropolitan police, who would surely have access to instruments of greater sensitivity. Thus decided, he strode out of the bridge to the cargo hold entrance, where he secured the *Cloudbreaker* against entry and turned for the captain's club. Thoughts of strong gin and hearty steaks occupied him, so he did not see the slim volume in his path until his foot struck it and sent it spinning across the deck. As he bent to pick it up, he recognized it as his captain's log.

"I'll be damned," Hardiman muttered as he lifted the book and flipped through its pages. His first thought was to wonder how it got here, but the answer was obvious. The real question was its placement here, and a few pages after his last entry, he discovered the answer. In a spiky, nearly feminine script, he discovered a message:

Your ship is a treasure, Captain. It was a joy and an honor to fly with her.

Hardiman read the two sentences again, then a third time. He looked around the loading deck and wondered where a stowaway could have been during the search. Then he looked down, pondering the latticework that stood between the deck plates and the streets far below, and thought of the skill and nerve it would take to leave this for him and risk discovery, much less climb under the deck and wait after six weeks alone, surviving on lifeboat rations and God knew what else, or find their way to an open window and escape inward and down to the streets. Someone like that would make a fine addition to Aerofleet, Hardiman thought. He smiled.

"Joy and honor, indeed," Hardiman said aloud, and left the *Cloudbreaker* at rest, docked in the night like a jewel tethered to the earth.

Brandon Nolta is a north Idaho-based writer, editor, tech geek, and member of both SFWA and Codex. His fiction, poetry and other scribblings have appeared in *Stupefying Stories*, *Amazing Stories*, *Digital Science Fiction*, *The Pedestal Magazine*, *New Myths*, *Tree and Stone,* and many others. His debut novel, *Iron and Smoke*, was published in 2015 by Montag Press; his second book, a collection of short fiction titled *These Shadowed Stars*, escaped in 2020.

Caliban's Cameras

By Allan Dyen-Shapiro

THE CONTACT GEL CHILLED PRINCIPAL CHANG'S TEMPLES. Worse, it failed to blunt the electrodes' cat-claw scratch. The visor snapped into place with faux-velour ovals positioned over his eyelids.

The salesman's stale breath warmed Chang's face. Trapped in the chair, Chang protested. "Please don't stand so close."

"Sorry."

The movement unblocked the draft from the ventilation system. In shirtsleeves, his customary blazer shed to avoid wrinkling from the restraints, Chang shivered.

"You may open your eyes."

Despite a double blink, darkness persisted. "I don't see anything."

"We haven't started yet. The peripherals are still auto-calibrating."

Unable to reposition his torso, Chang shifted his legs, struggling to minimize discomfort. A thick metal belt clamped his six-foot torso to the office couch, which pressed on his back in the wrong places. His oversized American flag fluttered a metronomic tap against the wall above his right ear. "So once we start, how long before we get output?"

Air circulation ceased as the salesman again drew close with a swish of polyester against polyester of trouser legs. No more taps. "Fifteen minutes maximum. Three hundred cameras, each recording for the same thirty seconds. Sequential connections then transmit all data in superfast mode. A jolt to your noggin releases drugs that allow all images to persist in your short-term memory.

The cycle repeats until you hit the capacity of your hypothalamus. You won't feel it." The salesman sprinted through his final claim with a don't-worry vibe.

Didn't work. Chang worried.

But he pressed on, probing for information. "And the parallel computing?"

"The human brain excels at parallel computing. It's the memory buffering that's crummy without advanced technology."

Chang folded his hands across his abdomen. "I don't like the instant reporting."

"None of the older principals do. But the people saw fit to elect the Florida Legislature, and they passed the revisions to the Sunshine Act. Do you have anything to hide?"

"No—"

"Then you're fine. Your brain will process the data from all security cameras, prioritize what's important, and post the report. It comes out of your mouth as gibberish, but the voice recorder captures it and converts it to a plain text file. Data is sent. You can read it when any citizen of Florida can."

Most citizens of Florida couldn't read. Sure, his kids scored well on the state tests, choosing the correct letter more often than not, earning him commendation. Certificates his wife had framed clung to and cluttered his office walls like barnacles encrusting a pier. But could he claim credit? He had chosen to purchase the text-to-animation software. Cartoon characters that acted out each question engaged the students, so fewer answered in a random fashion.

Some accomplishment. The Ed Chang who'd commanded a standing ovation for his community theater *Hamlet*, the Ed Chang who'd snuck *Macbeth* into the curriculum even for the lowest students, the Ed Chang who'd clawed his way into school administration prepared to fight for the kids—what happened to that guy?

A bell dinged.

"Peripherals ready to transmit." The salesman employed his much-practiced crescendo of voice with phased-in carny barker intonation. "Three hundred cameras with fifteen minutes of video and audio each, and you can digest it all in near-real time. It's breakthrough technology, better than anything else on the market. You can't monitor your school without this system. At least, not to the degree the legislature deems public interest. And you certainly don't want to risk being dismissed from your job for under-reporting. Ready?"

No, not at all. But he'd go through with the demo. If he were to fight this travesty, to win one last battle for the kids before he retired, he'd have to speak with authority when he confronted the Legislature in Tallahassee. To rally his fellow educators, to gain the public's sympathy, to gainsay the industry claims of benign utility, he needed to learn what he was up against. "Go ahead."

Footsteps on the wooden floor echoed as the breeze resumed. A switch clicked.

Chang cringed, his last conscious thought of Prospero's daughter.

Tap.

A mousy girl with round-rim spectacles stands at the end of a hallway, pouts, and swishes her behind for the benefit of those who stare. "Your finger smells."

"Been in my twat. You want to lick it?" The black leather-clad gang girl bats her eyelashes.

"Your finger or your twat?" The mousy girl rolls her tongue across her lips.

"You're cute."

Tap.

The special boy boards the freight elevator and runs his fingers over the coarse cloth that drapes the metal walls. He steps onto the empty pallet. "Wheee!"

Just before the door closes, another boy leaps in. "You're not going anywhere in this elevator, and this isn't a skateboard anyway, you retard."

"Fff...fff...fff..."

"What's the word you're trying to say? Does it mean copulate? Do the nasty? Stick your little man in someone's bunghole? Or is someone penetrating your behind? Speak, retard."

"Fff...fff...fff..."

"Fairy dust and falderal and other crap they tell you. Faintly fetching Fallon forced five Finnish firemen—"

"Fff...fff...fff..."

The unspecial boy pushes the red button to stop the elevator mid-floor.

Tap.

A gray-haired gentleman dressed in a button-up shirt with a bowtie hefts a green felt-covered rectangular box half his size onto a desk. "This is two X." With a grimace and trembling of arm muscles, he pulls the top half of the box to chest height. "The bottom is X, the top is X." A metallic click accompanies the reattachment of the two pieces. He exhales.

From within a sack, he pulls a fuzzy blue ball and places it next to the joined green object. He tosses three more to a student in the front row, who smiles.

"Two X plus three equals the one in Yeili's hand. How can we figure out what X is?"

Dead silence.

"X is not very friendly. X wants to be alone. Yeili, what could you take from me to help X be all by itself?"

She tightens her grip on the ball. "Why you picking on me?"

The teacher smiles. "Because I like you and you're very smart."

Most of the class dozes.

"Can anyone help Yeili out?" A minute passes. "Let's watch the same thing on the Magic System."

Depression of a button on the teacher's remote control calls forth an explosion of light and the sound of thunder. The students who'd been sleeping open their eyes. Holograms of green boxes and blue balls dance into formation. A ball disappears from each side of a giant equals sign. A moment later, half the green object and one of the balls disappear. "What was X?"

Dead silence.

Yeili tosses a ball to the teacher. "Yo, teach, was this how they taught this stuff to you? 'Cause it don't mean nothing to any of us."

"No, that was Mandatory Instructional Strategies number one and two. Number three is a game." He looks out at a sea of rolling eyes. "But this is how I learned it." He walks behind his desk, opens a drawer, and pulls out a dry erase marker. After writing the equation on the board, he demonstrates subtraction of one and division by two.

"So the answer is one?" Yeili asks.

"Yes!" The teacher beams with delight and claps.

A boy from the second row raises his hand and is recognized. "I like this way better. It makes sense. What do they call this method?"

"It used to be called teaching."

Tap.

The fishbowl on the counter overflows with condoms, each wrapped individually.

"Protection, we distribute it freely in this clinic," the school nurse, a beefy man sporting a *Semper Fi* t-shirt, says. He looks up from his computer to find the next in line paying no attention. A glare elicits assistance from the girl in the second position.

When she taps the boy's shoulder, he looks up from his dog-eared copy of Dostoevsky. She repeats the nurse's words.

"Protection from what?"

The nurse grins. "A virgin, eh? You bought into the abstinence crap? They paid me to push abstinence. Brought me close to drinking absinthe. Then the feds erased that budget line item." He glares at the boy. "You still listening? Protection from the nasties. The creeping rot you get when you stick it in dirty places. Didn't the programs scare you? How dare you ask protection from what?"

He stands and advances toward the boy. "Last chance butt-wipe. Why are you not scared?"

"Sorry sir, I'm hard of hearing. My individualized education plan calls for assistive technology to overcome my disability. I don't read lips well. Scared of what?"

Tap.

"My individualized education plan very clearly states I am to receive accommodations. Why are you not accommodating me?"

The teacher fumbles through folders. "You're not on the accommodations list."

"I'm telling my parents you didn't know my accommodations."

The teacher scoots his desk chair over to his computer, inputs the student's name and clicks search. Nothing. "The computer doesn't have your accommodations either."

"My Dad is buddy-buddy with the superintendent. They play tennis every Wednesday."

The teacher hits the emergency call button.

A disembodied voice intones from overhead: "What's your emergency?"

"I need to know Sanjay's accommodations. He says I'm not accommodating him."

Static crackles before the voice continues. "I'll get the

Assistant Principal."

The boy smiles. "Assistant Principal's my dog. I hang out in his office all the time. Your ass is grass, mister."

"You just got yourself a referral for profanity." The teacher pulls up the requisite form on his computer.

A new voice interrupts, again noncorporeal but this time omnipresent and commanding. "Mister Jenkins. What is it you want this time?"

The teacher fumbles and stumbles through lines and missives.

Dismissive, the boy butts in, "Mister Jenkins is trying to tell me I'm special ed. I keep telling him I don't need accommodations. I think he's smoking illegal stuff. Can you set him straight, sir?"

"Mister Jenkins, see me in my office."

Tap.

Seated in an otherwise empty stairwell, a lanky boy folds the dried leaves into paper, runs his tongue across, and creases it closed. He offers it to a frizzy-haired girl in a black t-shirt.

"Thanks." she says. "Can you flash me a light?"

He extracts a book of matches from his pocket, strikes one. The joint's near edge catches fire; she puffs on the other.

"Wicked." She pulls another drag and passes it to him.

"What are we doing here?" The security guard raps his palm with a black stick. "I caught you on camera."

She smiles. "Well you better erase it, because we stole one of the cameras and caught you with the janitor in the supply closet. You want the video on YouTube?"

"How...well...what—"

"And your dick is tiny. Is that what you want the world to see?"

He contemplates. "Okay. Finish quickly, please. I'll erase it." He leaves.

Her beau gazes in awe and wonder. "How did you think to put a camera in the supply closet?"

She giggles. "I didn't. But he thinks I did. You want to help me design his new Facebook page?"

Tap.

A twenty-something teacher seated behind her desk clicks at her mouse. "The website displayed on all of your screens identifies the Florida State Standards we will cover today. The words will turn a sparkly blue color when we have completed our learning to the degree specified by the State Legislature. Min-Jae, please read the standards for the class."

The young man pushes his glasses back from the tip of his nose. "Lit 3.21.RJ-17: The student will learn from the example of Capulets and Montagues that dissent from social norms leads to violence. Lit 3.21.RJ-18: The student will learn from the Veronese gentleman Capulet's willingness to consider marriage for his daughter Juliet, who has 'not seen the change of fourteen years,' to be aware that foreigners may be pedophiles. Lit 3.21.RJ-19…"

Tap.

The young woman opens the envelope. She thumbs through the green. She sobs. "I can't take this. You have a family—"

"Take it, Angelie. You have such promise." Her science teacher leans against the demonstration table and fingers the gas outlet absently.

Angelie bites her lower lip. Clinging to the envelope with both hands, she angles her head downward.

"You're the best student in my classes this year. If a little money can bail you out of a jam—"

"It's more than a little money, Ms. Hanes."

"You're worth it."

The student's lip quivers. "I'll never forget this." She throws her arms around the older woman. She soaks her teacher's blouse with tears.

Ms. Hanes pats her on the back. "It's not such a big deal. I had one when I was your age; I didn't want to be a teenage mom any more than you do. I finished school, established myself in my career, got married and had three wonderful kids. You've got all this to look forward to."

After releasing her teacher's embrace, Angelie inserts the envelope into her purse. From the open handbag, she extracts a pill bottle and hands it to Ms. Hanes. "Please throw these away."

In silence, Ms. Hanes examines the label.

"You don't need to file a report. I won't kill myself." She looks her teacher in the eye. "Really, I'm fine now. It was a stupid thought. This money will make everything okay. Thank you so much." She hugs Ms. Hanes again.

Angelie steps several paces toward the door, pauses and pivots to face the older woman. "Nobody's ever done anything like this for me. I'm so happy. I want to be just like you when I grow up. I want to be a teacher."

A smile graces her mentor's lips. "I think you'll be great."

The praise elicits a deep blush. "And of course I won't tell anyone about this. I know helping me could get you in big trouble. I promise you, no one will ever know."

Tap. Tap. Rip.

Chang jolted awake as the salesman tore off the mask. The room spun like a cyclone, and an acid taste burned the back of his throat.

Jumbled images faded, leaving his office, with its familiar leather and wood furniture. The throbbing in his head subsided.

"I've sent the summary file to your desktop. Peruse." The salesman handed Chang a stack of papers. "Then sign this contract at the yellow marks and initial at the green."

I must obey, his art is of such power.

"What was that? You mumbled."

"Shakespeare."

"Is he a student?"

Was his smile irony or idiocy? Chang couldn't tell and had wearied of conversation. To get rid of the fool and his neon-highlighted paperwork—so Chang could unwind, process this experience and focus his anger into a speech for the Legislature— Chang mustered his remaining civility. "Can you come back another day? I need a chance to look this over."

The salesman agreed, and with an *adiós*, exited.

Before Chang could close the office door, his secretary shouted for him to wait. "Principal Chang, the boys in the elevator—you need to see the footage."

"Whatever it is, I'll watch it later."

The secretary hyperventilated, barely able to speak. "At least approve the emergency call. System won't phone 911 without your biometric access code. I needed you but you were plugged in." She sniffled. Tears flowed like rivulets, eroding her mascara, muddying her cheeks.

She presented him with a rectangular pad.

Chang proffered his fingerprints. Once she departed, he shut the office door.

The light switches clicked as he depressed them in unison. He stumbled in the darkness to his desk chair and sank into the fine leather. He ran his fingers over the varnish on his antique wood desk. Smooth.

He snuck his hand into the bottom right drawer. Adeptly, he felt for the glass and bottle concealed underneath the hanging files. He decanted, sipped, and gulped. After tossing back a second drink, he closed his eyes.

They snapped open at the beep of his computer monitor. Red faux-cursive writing materialized against a black background. *Did*

I tell you the cameras were equipped with infrared sensors?

"You can hear me too, can't you?"

The word "yes" appeared. The text rotated, blinked, and jetted off the screen.

Chang waited. More words appeared on the screen. *Shall we delete this footage?*

At the price of a principal's soul.

The educator yearned to scream out into the black. The administrator caved. "I'll swear upon that bottle to be thy true subject; for the liquor is not earthly."

No response from the computer.

"Shakespeare? *The Tempest?*"

An audio response this time. "Sign the damn contract."

Chang did. He poured another drink.

Allan Dyen-Shapiro is a Ph.D. biochemist currently working as an educator. He's sold stories to numerous markets including *Dark Matter Magazine*, *Flash Fiction Online*, and *Grantville Gazette*. He also co-edited an anthology of SFF set in the Middle East. He is a member of SFWA and Codex. You can find links to his published stories (and some freebies) as well as his blog, where he opines on matters of interest to those who might like his fiction (environmentalism, futurism, science, literature, and science fiction in all media), at allandyenshapiro.com. Follow him on Twitter (@Allan_author_SF) and Mastodon (@Allan_author_SF@wandering.shop); friend him on Facebook (allandyenshapiro.author).

There Is Another Sky

By Bo Balder

JONES WALKED ALONG THE BEACH WITH HER BORROWED DOG. An early sliver of sun glinted off the space elevator being built in Sydney bay. The nanobots were busy shaping it from carbon tubes for maximum strength. It would lift up the heavy loads into a low orbit, where the space pendulum could grab them for their final swing into space.

The damn dog, a sweet but stupid Golden Retriever called Delicious, started barking like a maniac, ears up, eyes wide. It took off for a large dark mass in the distance. A beached whale, maybe? Or a dead one. Maybe it needed help.

Jones plowed after Delicious through the thick dry sand. As she came closer to the whale, several people hurried in the opposite direction pinching their noses. The next step made it clear why.

The stink was like a wall. The whale must be very, very dead.

Jones didn't have the luxury of moving away like a sensible person. She had to get the dog out of there.

"Delicious! Come to Jones!" she called, but the dog pretended not to hear, crazy with excitement. It sniffed the whale, ran off to bury its nose in the sand, then returned to bark and take another face-full of what must be rotting flesh. Jones took off her shirt and tied it before her mouth and nose. The stink was so bad her eyes teared up. "Delicious, come to mama!"

The dog didn't react. Jones had to move closer. The dead whale lay gleaming blue-green under the strengthening light. It had a very odd pointy snout, and its clawed feet still moved. Feet? Claws?

It wasn't a whale. Not even a dead one.

It was an alien.

Jones opened up a messenger window to the Sydney government, sending a photo and a text asking them to find out what it was and get it off the beach. They'd need large tractors. Or a flotilla of helicopters. It was enormous. And if it was still alive, whatever it was, it might need to get back to the ocean.

A gash in the thing's side dripped blue fluid. It had so many feet. And also mouths. With every step Jones took, her limited knowledge of large sea creatures wobbled harder. Man o' War? Kraken? ATK, the All The Knowledge base, denied them all. Unknown. She posted it up on a What Creature website, and excited non-answers flooded in. Nobody knew.

Bugger. She pulled the photo, but it was too late. This was no Earth creature. It was an alien and she'd just told the world about it.

Another message to the governor. *Keep people away from it. Cordon it off.* She created an emergency project and opened up bids to man it while she circled the alien whale at a respectful distance. The governor of Australia messaged her with a new secret bandwidth for her project. "Whatever you need, Jones," the governor said.

"Tnx ," she sent and made a grab for the stupidest dog in Oz.

Delicious whined. The dog's tongue was blue and its back felt floppy and loose as Jones dragged it out of the stench zone. Jones was about to propose it for a Darwin Award when she remembered that the marriage group and Marianne wouldn't thank her for getting the dog sick or worse on her first outing. She asked for a vet.

When about a thousand vets from all over the world answered in the first minute, she delegated picking the right one to her friends and colleagues Donnie McDonald and Poppy Kwan, who were the best headhunter and project manager she knew. They'd worked together before. This was getting out of hand in record time.

Delicious whined and sank down on trembling haunches. Her blue, slime-coated tongue hung out of her mouth. Jones stroked the fur, careful not to touch the places matted with slime. Poppy texted her that the vet was being brought in by helicopter, but would have to wait for hazmat suiting before he went in, as per the governor's order.

Since Jones had proposed these orders, she could hardly protest. But she needed to help the dog before it died under her hands, poor dumb thing. She could at least get the slime off. She put her shirt back on so the slime would at least have some barrier before it touched her skin and carried Delicious to the ocean. The dog squeaked pitifully but calmed down as the surf washed slime off her paws.

Jones' shirt went off again. She tore it in two and bound it around her hands so she could wash the dog. She pushed Delicious' head down so she could hang her tongue in the water. Salt water might not be safe to drink, but it had to be better than whatever was poisoning the dog.

A helicopter landed several hundred meters away on the sand. A figure in bright green suit started towards her. Jones found his ID in Poppy's file and texted him to hurry up.

Delicious had gone very quiet now. Jones couldn't tell, through the roaring of the surf, the wind, and the thick wet fabric around her hands if the dog was still alive. She kept stroking her so the poor thing would feel the comfort of her hands at least.

The green-clad vet came stumbling over the rough sand and sank to his knees beside Delicious. He opened the dog's mouth and put a tube into her throat.

Jones gave him some distance to let him work. More green-clad people were on their way towards her. Poppy's mails told her they were a doctor, another vet, a microbiologist, and a pollution chemist.

She took more steps away from Delicious and the vet. Nothing more she could do now for the dog. There were bigger problems to tackle. Since she was already exposed, she might as well take another look at the beached alien corpse. She remembered its legs moving. It could have been the movement of the surf, but she should check.

More and more vehicles and helicopters arrived as she headed back to the alien whale. Good. The outer cordoning was done, and the experts were arriving in droves. Her co-worker Donnie was busy setting up quick and dirty selection protocols to help Poppy. Who wouldn't want a part of this?

Jones wasn't so sure. She'd been thinking of her future, of her personal life, and if she died here, which wasn't unlikely, she'd never have the chance to hold her own child or get to know a dog. Or anything, for that matter. She sent an email apology to the marriage group and Marianne. Maybe her job just wasn't suited for a stable home life. Maybe she should find another line of work. All these crisis management jobs she'd taken on lately seemed to be funneling her into a dangerous kind of specialty.

The whale was now close enough for the stench to intensify again. Closer than before. She must be getting used to it. But let's face it, a stench was not air, it was particles in the air, and everything coming out of that alien corpse might be toxic.

Pants off and over her nose and mouth. She texted Poppy to get her a suit. Poppy sent back that it was on its way, and that Jones would, sadly, have to be quarantined. Jones answered with a demand for an office to be set up right here on the beach, so she could keep working.

She'd better hurry before the quarantine people showed up and shut her in a plastic tent. She was exposed anyway; she might as well gather intel. The creature loomed up dark blue against the frothy waves under the now fully risen sun. Jones walked back and forth at the tip of the blue beast. It was enormous, rising five or six meters into the air. Was this its snout or its back? She couldn't find eyes, just tendrils that might have waved if the creature was still alive.

"Can you hear me?" she asked, feeling foolish but determined to make at least an attempt at communication. "Wave a tendril if you can. Or stomp a paw."

She stomped her feet on a patch of clean wet sand. Water filled them at once. The tide was rising. The creature might be washed away soon. She frowned. If it kept leaking possibly toxic fluids, that wouldn't be good for the marine life in New Sydney Bay.

She texted Poppy again for more helicopters used for heavy lifting, so they could keep the alien from slipping back into the sea.

A news item flashed in a corner of her eye screen. A call for thousands of workers for a forest replanting, a much coveted work posting. Another one for a river bed clearing. She'd attended projects like this every summer of her schooling, but it seemed a bit early in the year. And then she twigged. This must be Donnie's work. He was starting the evacuation of New Sydney in this brilliant, low-key way. Most people loved attending big drives like that, ocean clean ups, forest replanting, river course shapings. It was hard work, but every night there were cookouts and parties and people made new friends and lovers by the droves.

She texted a thanks to Donnie and got a big, lurid grin back. She wished Donnie and Poppy could join her in the flesh, the big red-haired man and the tiny woman, but since that would expose them, it probably wasn't going to happen.

Back to work. She'd tried talking to the alien. That hadn't worked. It might not even have ears. She couldn't spot any eyes either, but what did she know about alien eyes? They might not look like Earth eyes at all. So she stood with legs spread, and held her arms in a big V. Then spread out wide. Then one up, one down. She wasn't saying anything, just trying to communicate to the creature that her actions were structured and deliberate. To give it the idea that she was sentient and would like to communicate. She needed experts.

She'd done audio and visual. It had to have some kind of senses, although maybe they were made for underwater communication instead of in the air? She scanned the sky for cargo helicopters, but nothing yet. They might have to be brought in from a long way away. Across the bay, she spotted Coast Guard vessels cordoning off the waters against the curious and the stupid.

Maybe she should stomp again.

She stomped twice. Then four times.

Another message. A certain B. Chavannes from Haiti, who identified himself as a mathematician, advised her to try a Fibonacci sequence. Haiti! The whole world was looking on. After looking up what a Fibonacci sequence was, Jones commenced stomping the start of a sequence, since the amount of stomps got large fast.

1, 2, 3, 5, 8, 13.

And again.

Did she imagine it or was there a movement in one clawed foot? Yes, there was. It was alive!

1, 2—and then the scratching on the sand petered out. It must be exhausted. Or dying. It needed help. What was keeping the experts?

At that point, everybody rolled in at once. Jeeps loaded with green hazmat suits drove over the beach. Their riders leaped out and grabbed Jones. Before she was bundled into the tent they were erecting, she spotted another team of hazmat suits surrounding the creature, taking samples, setting up lights, pumps, and then the tent flap came down.

Jones was directed to a stretcher, given blood tests, cognition tests, everything tests.

Through Poppy she was kept up to date with what was happening to the creature. The xenolinguists had progressed through the Fibonacci sequence to yes, no and undecided. It would take no more than a couple of hours before they knew why it was here and where it had come from. Meanwhile, xenobiologists were trying to find out what was wrong with it, make it comfortable, and heal it if possible.

Delicious was reported to be still alive, but not doing that well. They'd amputated her tongue and ordered a new one, but worrisome problems were occurring throughout the dog's body.

From the frowns on the masked faces around her, Jones gathered that the results on her own health weren't that great either. She was feeling fine, so far, but she guessed that didn't mean much.

§

Her eyelids wouldn't open. Her right arm hurt when she tried to move it, so she rubbed out the gunk with her left hand. The light in the tent seemed dimmed, and machines beeped softly. She asked the machines for her status and read the results with growing disbelief. She'd nearly died. Alien infection. Coma. She didn't remember passing out, but she must have. Sitting up hurt, and then she discovered tubes in her arm and throat. Just knowing this started up a gag reflex and after a couple of unpleasant minutes, the slimed tube dropped from her mouth.

She was feeling fine. Why did the status say otherwise? The machines around her still pronounced her in deep coma, heart rate and blood pressure dangerously low.

Was she having an out of body experience? Jones pinched herself. It hurt, so this was real. Also, she stank.

And although she was feeling fine, she did feel different. To start with, she sensed she wasn't alone. A couple dozen feet north, there was someone else of her. And to the south, there were very many of her, and those were in distress.

That was new, and pretty scary. There had only ever been one Jones. Humans didn't come in groups. She rubbed her hand over her face and hair. Everything felt like always. What she could see of her body looked intact and complete. But the weird, displaced feeling remained.

She had to know what those other pieces of her were.

Jones swung her legs off the bed. Her feet landed on sand. Of course, she was still on the beach, in quarantine. With her feet on the ground her mind felt sharper instantly. She could guess now what the extra pieces of Jones were. One was Delicious, poor thing, and the other must be the dying alien on the beach.

She peeked under her clothes, shook her head, stomped her feet. Still her regular self. Her sickbed status indicated alien cells had nestled inside her like cancer, destroying her body. That might still be true, but she felt alert and energized by an urgency that must be coming from the alien.

First she needed to escape from her confinement. For all the peace and quiet, she knew the beach must still be quarantined and chock full of doctors and biologists, maybe even hastily deputized military people. Right. She needed the dog, and then to get closer to the alien. It was important.

An email dinged in. It was from Poppy Kwan and read: "I saw from your vitals that you're awake. I hired someone to fake your stats so you could get out of there undetected. Did I do right?"

"Pops, you're the best PA ever. Wish you were here in person. Tell me where they keep Delicious. This whole area is digitally invisible."

"Tell me about it. I'm hacking into the specially tasked satellite. Delicious is in an adjoining tent. Yours should have two exits, one orange, one green. Take the green one."

"Can't see colors in the dark. But I think I see the one you mean."

"Jones, it's bright daylight. You sure you're all right?"

Jones looked up at the tent's transparent roof. It was dark. Although there was something brownish, like a rotting tangerine, hanging in the sky just below zenith. That was upsetting.

Something was going on with her, that was for sure. Only she couldn't think what. But first things first.

Walking felt funny. Her soles didn't really want to touch the dry sand, it was sucking the moisture out of her feet. She should have put on sandals. Or had she? She had to look to make sure. No, bare feet. Onwards.

Inside the adjoining tent, as deserted as hers, she found Delicious, lying limp and lilac-tinged on her own doggy hospital bed, complete with beeping monitors. This was good. She stretched out her hand to touch Delicious, and made contact at once. The dog understood and complied. They needed to get closer to the alien, the two of them.

The urgency she felt must be the alien's. Maybe the communication could be two-way. She tried to reassure it, but felt nothing in return. Maybe because she only had a few alien cells, and the whale had trillions.

"Pop, can you do the same for Delicious as you did for me? Faking the stats?"

"Already done," Poppy sent back. "Are you sure this is the right thing to do? You were sending me emails before you were awake, according to the monitor."

Jones didn't remember that. But it probably didn't matter.

Other things were more pressing.

She detached Delicious from her tubes and set the dog on her feet.

"The alien's tent is through the blue zippered door, and down a short interior hall," Poppy sent. "You're all sealed in the same air-locked complex. There are scientists working around the alien's head or what they think is a head. I'll guide you to the midsection."

"Bless you, Poppy."

Jones felt she should stop and think about what she was doing, but her body moved to enter the alien's tent. She noted the split with a sense of foreboding. Not a whole lot of free will left, apparently.

The body of the whale took up most of the vertical space of the tent, but on the sides there was some room to maneuver. Jones' body didn't waste time maneuvering and simply plunged head and hands into the blubbery bluish mass that was the alien.

Now she was fucked.

Something rough and slippery at the same time wiggled against her right palm. After what seemed like ages of slow thought, she realized it was the dog's head. She slid her hand down until she felt its collar. They were both lost inside an alien and could use the support.

"What do you want?" she thought.

She waited for the answer.

None came.

It hadn't been her question, but the alien's.

"To help you," she said. "Are you ill? Where did you come from?"

The alien responded with a movie-like sequence. It showed something large and purple falling apart and covering an orange in purple goo.

With the molasses speed of dreams, Jones pieced the answer

together. The alien was dying and/or falling apart, and would cover the world in itself.

That didn't seem good.

Before Jones could proceed with her own thoughts, another movie started up. She went down down down into the sea until it was too dark to see anything, too cold to think and the pressure made everything silent. There, in a groove on the side of a deep trench, an alien ship rested. Maybe forgotten, maybe left to survey the Earth, but it stayed there for a very long time, thousands or millions of years.

The sea bottom shook. The trench cracked and the ship broke. Its inhabitant spewed out, forced to rise up by gases from its ship and its own splintered body.

Jones' thoughts expanded as the movie's images withdrew. Wow. An alien from outer space, marooned and dying, out of its element.

The image of the purple goo covering the globe returned.

Jones got it. The alien was dangerous. If its body broke down further, its particles would spread over Earth and endanger or even kill its inhabitants. It could recall its parts as long as it was alive, but after its death, it would spread and multiply for a long time before it would try to reorganize itself. The cycle of its life.

"What can we do about that?" she asked. "No wait, I want to know your name. I'm Jones and this is Delicious."

The image or taste Jones received seemed best translated into something like Purple Emanation. A beautiful name for something deadly dangerous and very ugly.

"I'm sorry. I didn't mean to think that. I'm sure you'd look great under your own kind of atmospheric pressure."

Amusement.

"So what needs to be done? How can we neutralize your danger?"

Jones didn't want to think it, but: "Burn your body?"

Jones tasted ash in her mouth as Purple Emanation recoiled from that thought. The purple goo still crept over the earth.

A hazy pencil shape, or a torpedo, no, a rocket trembled in the orange twilight that was Purple's perception of sunlight. The rocket took off from a small globe, presumably the Earth, and went into space.

"Do you want to go back home?" Jones asked.

Purple didn't give a clear answer. Jones senses loss and longing, but also regret and resignation.

"But you need to get off the Earth so you won't kill us all."

Yes, that was it. And us meant not just humans, but all creatures on this Earth. No living thing would survive the changes the goo would make. Nothing.

"I got it. Let me go and talk to my people to make this possible. They're not prepared for this. How much time do we have?"

Jones received uncertainty. The rotting orange of the sun dimmed and brightened a few times, but it didn't feel conclusive. But it was clearly five to midnight already.

Like a snap of an elastic band, the alien's consciousness sprang away from her own. Jones fell backward, leaving the alien body with a plop. She vomited purple.

Purple Emanation had had her say. Jones needed to find the solutions on her own.

§

Jones and Delicious staggered toward the alien's head. She was met by a circle of hazmat suits, with actual guns trained on her. She lifted her hands. "I talked to the alien. She's called Purple Emanation. We need to get her off the Earth or she'll fall apart and pollute the ocean." That seemed like a plausible and dangerous scenario, without the doom and paralysis that would accompany the larger narrative.

Her statement didn't immediately result in a great flurry of action. Jones was prepared to repeat it many times over several hours while she regained control over the operation. If she did. Poppy's reports weren't optimistic. Donnie had been arguing with the governor, and in fact they were both waiting for her. Only no one would be allowed within a hundred yards of her.

"I'm no longer contaminated," Jones told them. "I vomited up all the alien cells."

This didn't help either in making the hazmats listen to her.

"Poppy, I'm fine. It's urgent. Don't let them cut off my connections, don't let them take the operation leadership away from me. We're in a hurry."

The hazmats didn't care about governments and politics. They checked her out, repeatedly and unpleasantly, while Jones fumed and tried to communicate with her aides. Poked, prodded, tapped for blood in unlikely places, and measured. At last a suit came in to check her memory. "Mother's maiden name. Father's name. Address."

Finally her operation command was reinstated, but at the same time her communications were cut off. The last message she received told her Donnie and Poppy had started work on the projects she'd requested. Ways to get the alien off Earth. Ways to contain or destroy it if they couldn't.

A new hazmat suit entered Jones's containment room. From its bulging, hulking stature and its apologetic shuffle she recognized Donnie.

"Jones! How are you feeling?"

"I'm fine. A little queasy because I had an alien in my head. What's the progress on the extradition?"

Donnie scratched his helmet. "From estimates about its weight, it's too heavy to get on a plane or shuttle. We could tug it to the South Pole, maybe, minimize the environmental damage."

"Can we destroy it? Fire? Acid?"

"They tried on bits they got out of the dog and the water, but that seems to trigger a multiplication of the alien proteins."

"That makes sense. Sadly. It told me it could contain the multiplication while it was still alive, but when it dies it falls apart, spreads out, starts multiplying until it's large enough and safe enough to become intelligent again. It'll be someone else."

"What's the timeline on that?" Donnie asked.

Jones could sense his dismay. She shook her head. "I don't know exactly. Thousands, ten thousands of years? That's not the solution."

"What if we cut it into smaller pieces that would fit into large cargo planes? I'm checking out old rockets that were used for supplying satellites."

"I think that will still kill it, and make it witless and dangerous." Jones rubbed her aching head. "Do you want me to go in again?"

Donnie grabbed her hand. "What exactly does 'go in' mean?"

"Drowning myself in the goo, basically. Letting it colonize me temporarily so we can communicate."

Donnie looked horrified. "You must be joking! Of course you're not doing that. God, is that what happened? How do you know that you're not still inhabited by mindless particles eating you up from the inside?"

Questions like that made Jones' skin tingle and bowels ache. "I don't know. I hope not. I don't think it's like a robber wasp. Sheesh, Donnie."

Jones stared at her screen, where Purple Em lay as a big green tent. Dots started to stipple the bay. "What are those?"

"Ships with cranes," Donnie said. "We found a whale hospital ship within reasonable distance. They're waiting for it and setting up a combined lifting platform."

"Whale hospital ship?" Jones said, trying to imagine such a thing.

"When whales were still endangered, Pacific governments banded together to help the remaining whales survive as long as possible. Treating wounds, helping with birthing." He handed her his tablet with a video clip of a giant blue whale being lifted out of the ocean in great webbing bands.

"That should do it, right?"

Donnie shrugged. "It's hard to estimate the alien's actual weight. Or its body's tensile strength. A whale has bones and tendons and muscles to keep its meat together. We don't know if the alien has anything like that."

Jones rubbed her brow. Her fingers ached to get back online and oversee things directly, but she was still shut off from the net. As if her thoughts and actions were as dangerously viral as her cells might be.

She went outside to watch red metal crane ships maneuvering like clumsy whales through Sydney Harbor. "What's the news?"

"The news is problems. The alien—"

"Purple Em."

"Purple Emanation is still beached. The ships can't get close enough."

Ten minutes later, helicopters flew in, schlepping bands of webbing beneath their bellies.

"They can't carry that weight, can they?" Jones asked. Donnie brought her a hat and sunglasses. Maybe a couple of beach chairs and a daiquiri might be in order. But the outcome was hardly certain yet.

The webbing looked to be attached. Jones grabbed Donnie's free, gloved hand to share her excitement. Donnie's flinch reminded Jones of her recent recovery.

"I'm sorry. Do you want to get checked out?"

Donnie shook his head. "I'm sorry for reacting that way. Just silly fear. I know you were checked out and pronounced goo-free. It's just…"

Jones understood.

"A message from Marianne, btw."

Jones felt her neck muscles cord. "Oh God, she's reaming me out about Delicious, right?"

Donnie mock bitch-slapped her. "No, you stupid woman. She's concerned about *you*. What's with the insane fears about the dog?"

Jones forced her face into more relaxed lines. "She's checking out a marriage group, I told you. Taking the dog for a run was like a test. Can I do anything normal without falling foul of terrorists, refugees, or aliens? The answer, clearly, is no."

Donnie shook his head. "I think that's part of your charm. Your ability to make waves, to help people. If Marianne doesn't appreciate that, I say ditch her."

The left screen went black and a woman's face took shape. Negative freckles, high cheekbones and close-cropped hair. Marianne. She smiled and waved. "Jones! I know we can't talk to you because you're quarantined, so we're sending this to Donnie. But I just wanted to tell you that we're all watching and rooting for you! Save Purple Emanation! Yay Jones!"

The camera zoomed out and showed the whole marriage group, five adults besides Marianne, and two children, smiling and waving.

Donnie coughed. He had his head turned away from Jones but she was pretty sure he was wiping his eyes. Sentimental bastard. But then again, her eyes were swimming as well, from being loved and relief from their forgiveness about the dog.

"Can I send something back?" she asked Donnie.

"Sure. I'll film. Smile and say something nice."

Jones composed herself. "Guys, Marianne, thank you so much for your message! It made my day. I don't know when I'll be able to see you, but we're working on sending Purple Em to space." She didn't mention that it would probably mean Em's death. The children didn't need to hear that, or maybe none of them did.

She returned her focus to the activity on screen. The webbing around Em tightened. Jones' face fell back into its stressed grimace. There was no point in stressing, no point... The helicopters' engine started to whine. That couldn't be good.

The whine rose in pitch.

"Tell them to cut and abort!" Jones yelled at Donnie.

"Don't micromanage," Donnie said between clenched teeth. "They know their jobs, better than you do"

The webbing fell back on Purple Em's body.

"Jesus. This is a disaster."

Donnie nodded, his eyes riveted on the stream of incoming reports. Jones wanted to be in on the information so badly her teeth ached. *Cut it out, Jones*, she told herself. *This is the best you're going to get, a trusted friend who will listen to your advice.*

She put her hat back on against the glare of the sun. A whole day gone.

Getting Em out whole was off the table. But that meant that they were going to have to cut her up, and how could they do that without her body going rampant? Jones wanted to get infected again and talk to Em. But if that had been useful, Em wouldn't have released her.

She stared over the water. The irregular outline of the space elevator stuck up out of the water, the growth rate invisible at this distance.

A faint notion budded in Jones' mind. "The Space Elevator.

It's being built by nano things, right? How do those things transport the building materials?"

Donnie raised his eyebrows. "The short answer, by eating them and excreting them. Do you want me to look it up?"

"Yes. Get some engineers online."

Jones stepped outside the tent to look at the shadowy outline of the elevator foot. The night was too dark to see it grow, as one supposedly could when looking at it in bright daylight.

"Donnie, see if they can build up a very tall but light tower in a couple of hours. I want the nanites to dismantle the alien and then blast it into space. Where it is free to reassemble itself if possible, or to die in peace and become stupid. We'll be safe from its poison."

"Hold on," Donnie said. His face flushed and his fingers were dancing in the air. "I hope you're right."

Donnie nodded to his invisible counterpart. "Yes. Can we do that? Well, forward me to someone who can answer that question."

He looked at Jones. "The web's lighting up with your notion. I think we can do it. We're rounding up programmers now."

He turned away and started talking and typing at the same time.

Jones sank down into the sand. It might work. It also meant that Purple Em was going to die. That was sad. She wished she could talk to Em again for one last time. But the risk was too great. Em wouldn't want that for her.

Donnie stuck up his thumb. "It's on, we're trying this."

Ships' engines started up and chugged to the Space Elevator which bubbled up out of the water like a slow volcano. A suited-up work team brought in external screens so Jones could watch the operation while she was still quarantined from the net.

That was nice, but then again, the thought of Em's fate made her throat feel scratchy and her eyes burned. Em would die. Jones had failed. She'd wanted to help the alien so badly.

But there was no choice, as Em herself had known. Better one dead alien than a ruined world. Especially Earth, which humankind had only just rescued from the brink of climate disaster. They couldn't run the risk of anything disturbing that delicate ecological balance again.

Shipboard cams went up. The footage from the elevator base streamed to the screens. At first Jones noticed no change in the fuzzy surface of the base. To her layman's eye, it looked like coral, beautiful but random.

She managed to stay functional enough to watch the progress at the elevator foot.

Donnie shook her shoulder. "It's working, Jones. The nanites are taking Em apart molecule by molecule."

Jones blinked gritty eyes. She was so tired. Donnie shoved something hot and grossly sweet up to her face and she managed to drink half of it. "What about the next step? How are we getting her into space? The elevator isn't finished. Can we use the one near Easter Island?"

Donnie shook his head. "Too far. But the transport up to the space station has been declared safe. They've cleared a dock for her there, which they can open out to space at a moment's notice, to see if she can assemble herself again."

"And you've got to see this." He gestured to one of the screens.

At first Jones couldn't make sense of the seething mass of silvery things, flickering and lighting up. But then she got it. At moments their lights flickered in unison. 1, 2, 3, 5, 8, 17, 28. The Fibonacci sequence she'd used to initiate contact with Em. "Wow. She's saying goodbye."

Wait, 17, 28? That made no sense. "She's breaking up. She's losing control."

The sequence started again. 1, 2, 3, 11, 1, 11, 1.

"Does that mean anything? Donnie?"

Donnie took her hand between his. He was wearing gloves, which was sensible of him, but the gesture still worked, especially since she knew he was scared of touching her. "She knew—knows we tried to save her. Let's hope she makes it."

Jones stared at the screened enlargement, where tiny robots scurried about in incomprehensible patterns. She'd never felt more distant from humanity. Why strive so hard to save one individual if it failed in the end?

Donnie's hand tugged her back down to Earth. "Jones. Earth to Jones? Look what just got delivered. Since we can't celebrate with the rest of New Sydney, this case of beer will have to do. Come on out to the beach. We can watch the sky without infecting the city."

Drone fireworks blossomed over downtown New Sydney. They blinked a Fibonacci sequence. Someone was being thoughtful.

"Maybe Purple Em will see it," Jones said.

"I'm sure she will," Donnie said. "Come on, fireworks, that's universal."

Jones drank her cold beer and wiped off her cheeks. She was very glad of his company, quarantine or not.

"Jones? I wouldn't worry about Marianne and the marriage group. Your heart is big enough to contain a giant alien. If I can see that, so can they."

Jones toasted with Donnie and lifted her plastic beer glass to the sky. "To Em! May you come together again, someday."

Bo Balder lives and works close to Amsterdam. Bo is the first Dutch author to have been published in *F&SF*, *Clarkesworld*, *Analog* and other places. Her sf novel, *The Wan*, was published by Pink Narcissus Press. When not writing, she knits, reads and gardens, preferably all three at the same time.

For more about her work, you can visit her website (boukjebalder.nl) or find her on Facebook or Twitter (@bo.balder)

Something Came Through

By Michael D. Burnside

WE INDEPENDENT SPACE JOCKEYS DON'T GET OFFERED WORK VERY OFTEN. It turns out that low-G environments constantly being bombarded by radiation are bad for humans. It's almost always easier to send a bot.

I'd been unemployed for a year and had grown desperate enough to consider applying to one of the low orbit tourist companies, even though I was certain hauling vomiting civilians around the globe would drain me of the will to live.

A bundle of overdue payment notifications arrived, and I considered my options. Did I really need an apartment? The interior of my leased car was roomier than some space station habitat modules I'd been forced to live in. On the other hand, maybe piloting low orbit tourist flights wouldn't be so bad. I'd be sealed off on the flight deck and wouldn't actually have to see anyone puke. But what if I was expected to help with the post-flight cleanup?

I was just about to call a tourist company with some pertinent questions about sanitation duty when my phone rang.

"Hello?" I said.

"Ryan Fernald?" asked a voice on the other end.

"Yeah."

"This is Steve Kern with Rosche Corporation. You did some lunar flights for us a few years back."

"That's right," I said.

"We're putting a crew together for a priority mission and I'd like you to be part of it. Are you available?"

"Absolutely." The excitement in my voice would probably cost me when it came time to negotiate my fee, but I was too happy about not becoming a tour bus driver to care.

§

I met the rest of the crew at Rosche's California facility. Meeting people is always awkward for me. Whenever I meet someone new, I always look into their eyes and wonder, *How big of a psychotic pain in the ass are you?* If the answer isn't good, it's no big deal with ordinary folks. I can always walk away. But with crew members, there's no walking away. When I meet new crew, I'm meeting people I'm going to be locked up with for months. It's like meeting new cellmates in prison.

And there's a bit of history that makes meeting new crew members even more awkward. For many decades, only married couples went on the long missions. A trip out to Mars used to take nine freaking months. May God bless the poor souls that first went out to Ceres, a trip of eight years. Now that the rockets have gotten better, the married couple requirement isn't as common, but there's still some pressure on the single folks to hook up with another single crew member for the mission. So as I shook the hand of a pretty blonde woman named Lena, my helpful brain thought, *Hey, how big of a pain in the ass are you?* and *Say, you wanna boink during the trip?*

The answers turned out to be, *Not that bad* and *Absolutely not*.

Lena was the medic for the mission. As an added bonus, she was also a fully qualified pilot, making her twice as useful as me. She introduced me to her wife, Claire, thus answering my question about the possibility of boinking without my ever having to ask it.

Claire was an engineer. She and Lena both wore their hair short, which could have just been a style choice, but I chose to take it as a sign they'd done some stints in space before. Long hair is a pain in the ass in zero-G. Most veterans tend to chop it off before a mission rather than have it float around in their face or subjecting it to vacuum clippers.

The last member of the crew strutted up to me and held out his hand. "Hey, I'm Rex."

And thus ended any chance of boinking on this trip. I started hoping it would be a quick lunar orbit and back.

"I'm Ryan." I said, and shook Rex's hand. He had a face that featured a chiseled chin. His hair was medium length and had too much product in it. When I looked into his eyes and my brain asked *How big of a pain in the ass are you going to be?* I instinctively knew the answer was, *Epic.*

The arrival of a small group of Rosche personnel put the awkward crew introductions on hold. We all took a seat around a large conference table as the Rosche mission planner launched into his briefing.

"Hey everyone, I'm Steve Kern. I'll be running things back here at base while you folks are soaring through the heavens." He gave me a quick wave. "Ryan, good to see you. Ryan Fernald here is our lead pilot. Lena Yor is our medical officer and assistant pilot. Her wife, Claire Yor, is our mission specialist. And Rex Helsberg is our mission commander."

Steve shuffled some notes and rubbed his chin. "I suppose you're all wondering just what the mission is. I take it you're all familiar with Bennett Station?"

A shivering thrill ran through me. Bennett Station? It was only the most amazing thing humans had ever built. In orbit around Mars, the station controlled a giant teleporter linked to the Alpha Centauri system. It had allowed humans to become an interplanetary species.

Actually, Bennett Station was the second most amazing thing humans had built. The first would be the exact same station but in orbit around Demory, a lifeless rock of a planet in the Alpha Centauri system. That station's official name was Wayfarer, but everyone always referred to it as the Alpha Centauri station. It had taken forty years of firing a massive laser at a space tug with a solar sail thousands of miles in diameter to get it into position. Bennett and the Alpha Centauri station formed a link with their massive teleporters allowing objects to be copied and transmitted instantly over a distance of 4.3 light years. For the first time, humans were able to send probes to another star system. The probes had discovered a paradise-like planet orbiting Alpha Centauri B, the medium-sized star in the trinary system. The planet was given the name Eden. Insanely brave humans, mostly insane, had allowed themselves to be teleported over to Alpha Centauri and had founded a colony on Eden, the first human colony outside our solar system.

So yeah, I was familiar with Bennett Station. I gave Steve a nod.

"A month ago, a scheduled cargo shipment from the Alpha Centauri station failed to arrive at Bennett." Steve frowned. "Communication packets sent through the transporter were not returned. A week ago, we lost radio contact with Bennett station. Your task is to head out there and get Bennett Station's communications gear back on line. Then, see if you can find out what's wrong with the teleporter."

My danger instincts should have kicked in. Hell, most horror stories have the words "and we've lost contact with" somewhere on the first page. But I was too excited about seeing the giant teleporter and got caught up in the importance of the job. No humans were posted full time on Bennett station. It was crewed by a bot and computers. The station was the only way the people on Eden could connect to Earth.

"How are we going to be able to diagnose any problems with

the teleporter?" I asked. As far as I was concerned, that thing worked on the basis of quantum mechanics magic and pixie dust.

"Rex has that covered," answered Steve. "Your mission commander worked on upgrading the system five years ago."

Rex gave me a wide smile.

"Great," I said. And I meant it. Rex being important to the mission would help me overcome the urge to toss him out an airlock.

"More good news," continued Steve, "Rosche is assigning a Falcon 50 anti-matter rocket to this mission. If we can launch within our scheduled window, your trip to Bennett Station will only take forty-five days."

That was good news. In fact, it was awesome news. I'd get to pilot the most advanced rocket ever. Due to the density of anti-matter, we'd have enough fuel to do a full burn halfway there, then turn around and decelerate for the other half. We'd have something akin to gravity the whole trip, which meant we'd feel a whole lot healthier once the mission was done.

Some folks worry about having anti-matter aboard a ship, but honestly, the most it can do is kill you. How is that any different than hauling around tons of explosive chemical propellant? Dead is dead. I don't worry about the risks I can't control. Anti-matter cuts transit time by half, so I love the stuff.

I figured forty-five days out, a month of work to repair one of the most incredible machines ever made, and then forty-five days back. I estimated the job would be done in four months if everything went smoothly.

Of course, nothing in my life ever goes smoothly.

§

Tucked beneath a monstrous scramjet, I felt like a field mouse being carried away by an eagle. Rex sat next to me in our orbital transfer pod. Lena and Claire sat below us on deck two.

There wasn't anything for me to do at this point except watch the instruments. The scramjet would get us going as fast and high as it could before we detached. The bulk of the scramjet's body blocked out the sun, but straight ahead I could see the sky darkening to black as we rode higher and higher.

We wore pressure suits just in case things went suddenly wrong, but had our helmets off and clipped to our seats. The ride was bumpy and loud and would only get more so once we detached.

The voice of the scramjet's pilot buzzed over the radio. "Altitude and speed achieved. Detach when ready."

"Roger, Mother Hen," I responded.

I reached up and toggled the safety release switches. Rex watched me like a hawk.

"Releasing on three," I said. "One. Two. Three." I pulled the release handle. We detached from the scramjet with a loud pop. I moved my hand over the rocket igniter switches while I watched the scramjet soar away from us.

Rex leaned over to me. "What's your plan here, Ryan?"

I raised an eyebrow. "Same flight path as in the simulator. Why?"

"I just want to be sure you're not planning on putting us through a few extra G's in an attempt to show off for the ladies."

"You're worried about me trying to impress our two women crew members? The ones who are married to each other?"

Rex nodded.

"No, I won't be trying to seduce our lesbian crew members by making them queasy. I'm just going to fly the pre-planned flight path."

"Good," said Rex as he sat back in his seat.

He'd been like this through all four weeks of mission training.

He was thorough and meticulous, which are qualities I want in a mission commander, but he didn't trust any of us to actually do our jobs.

And he'd distracted me at a critical moment. We were well clear of the scramjet and losing speed.

"Engaging rockets," I announced and flipped the engage switch without any countdown. "Rocket engagement was late. We'll have to burn a few extra seconds."

Rex glared at me. I glared back.

§

Once in orbit, we docked with the Falcon 50. This particular ship was named *Asimov's Dream*, and she was a beauty. She reminded me of a Roman column used in ancient temples, except with a rounded top and an engine nozzle on the bottom.

The habitable area of the ship made up only about a third of the ship's length. There was a large amount of shielding between the crew compartment and the engine to block the gamma rays that the anti-matter reaction produced. Still, the amount of room we had wasn't bad. We had two crew compartments, the flight deck, and a general use area that could be used for exercise, dining, or surgery.

Lena and Claire got one of the crew compartments and, lucky me, I got to room with Rex.

We transferred our gear and supplies to the Falcon and sent the orbital transfer pod back to Earth. Then we all strapped in as I entered our navigation plan into the computer and prepared to ignite the anti-matter rocket.

Rex double-checked everything I did, which I would have insisted he do if he hadn't. It would have been embarrassing and potentially fatal to go zooming off in the wrong direction. But after the incident on the flight to orbit, everything he did irritated me.

I told myself if I just kept my composure professional, this mission would zoom right by, but the cynical side of my brain said I was lying. The mission was going to drag. Rex was going to be criticizing my sleeping bag's restraint lines while I had to listen to the sounds of an amorous couple across the hall.

The anti-matter rocket was capable of pasting us into our seats, but we wanted a nice steady burn rate. Our flight plan gave us a comfortable single G for the duration of the trip. I ignited the rocket, and we were on our way.

§

It turned out I need not have worried about having to listen to lovemaking while I endured celibacy because our married couple fought the whole way to Mars. If you ever have the choice between staying with an overly affectionate couple and a couple bound for a breakup, choose the affectionate couple. Sure, the giggling and cutesy pet names will make you nauseous, but you don't end up feeling bad for anyone except yourself.

Claire and Lena did a fine job of keeping their work professional and separate from their private troubles, which actually made it worse for me. If one of them had acted like a raging asshole, I could have just boxed that person off in my brain in the area I reserved for jerks, like Rex, and moved on with just enduring them till the mission was over. But they both seemed to be decent people who did their jobs well and just happened to be in a relationship that was failing. I felt bad for both of them.

Meanwhile, Rex was driving me crazy.

If you've never seen the inside of a spacecraft equipped for a long-range mission, let me paint you a picture. There's stuff everywhere. Eight months of food were tied to the walls. Spacesuits hung from the ceilings. Emergency water packs were crammed into every cubby hole. The ship held tools, gadgets, pumps, a vacuum hair cutter, a foldout table, a kitchen sink featuring a vacuum drain, an emergency stretcher, emergency lamps, emergency heaters… Basically what I'm saying is there's a lot of stuff. And Rex was right when he said everything had to have a place, however, as I told him—"I have to pee several times a day and with the grace of God we won't ever need to use the emergency water filtration system, so why not secure that tank somewhere else instead of having to haul it out of the way every time I have to go?"

"Because if we move it, we might forget where we put it, and we'd have to move something else to make room for it and then we forget where we put that," said Rex.

I pointed at the cluster of spacesuits. "We could suspend it from that rack. The suits are flexible. We could make it fit without having to move anything else."

Rex shook his head. "I don't want that kind of weight up there."

"Up is relative. It'll be down once we turn around. It's just a matter of securing it properly."

"It's secured properly right now," argued Rex.

"Not when I'm peeing it's not. Suppose the engine shuts down while I'm using the bathroom? It'll go flying. It's got enough mass to ruin someone's day if it hits them."

"The probability of that happening is low. If you're too lazy to move the tank, use the bathroom in the ladies' compartment. It's always unobstructed."

I didn't want to go invading the privacy of our married couple, but I didn't raise that objection because I knew Rex wouldn't care. He was a by-the-book guy even when the book wasn't practical. I cursed under my breath and left our shared crew compartment.

In the common area there was a large window. The constant acceleration meant you had to climb up to it, but once there you could make a cozy seat from the laundry bags secured around it. It was the perfect spot to look out at the stars and cool my temper.

Unfortunately, on this day it was already occupied by Lena.

I thought about just leaving her be, but I really needed to get away from Rex, so I climbed up anyway. As I sat down on a bag, I asked, "Mind if I join you?"

Lena looked away from the window and stared at me with big blue eyes. Tears ran down her cheeks.

I started to get up. "Oh, crap. I'm sorry."

She grabbed my wrist. "No. Please stay. I need someone to talk to."

I didn't want to get in the middle of a domestic dispute, but couldn't see any way of escaping that wouldn't hurt Lena's feelings. I let out a drawn out, "Okay" and slowly sat back down.

"Do you ever get scared?" asked Lena.

"Scared of what?"

"Being so far from home, of screwing up, of the future, of anything…"

"Well, there was this one time I was waiting on a paternity test. I'd only learned the young lady in question was a kleptomaniac arsonist after I slept with her so… Okay, so I actually knew beforehand, but she was hot. But definitely not someone I wanted to get tied down with cause she seemed the type who would take all my stuff and burn it. So that was pretty scary."

"I'm being serious," said Lena.

"So am I," I said. "I used to have nice stuff."

"Used to have?"

"Well, the test turned out negative, but my suspicions about her turned out positive."

She shook her head slightly and gave me a small smile. Her blond hair had gained some length in the weeks since we left. She looked stunning sitting there, silhouetted by the stars.

She looked back out the window and said, "I've never been this far from Earth before. Claire and I have done plenty of lunar hops. On those you get to see Earth multiple times a day. I remember my first orbit around the backside of the moon. It looked like an ancient battlefield, all cratered and gray. But then you see it—the curve of the moon, and hanging behind it in the darkness is that beautiful blue planet. Right there is home."

She looked back at me. "I haven't seen home since we engaged the engines."

"It's behind us," I said. "We're chasing Mars. I can show Mars to you from the flight deck if you want to see it."

She shook her head. "It's not home. I don't like being out this far. I liked the lunar missions. That's about as far from Earth as I wanted to go. But Claire has this plan. We started by working the tourist Earth orbits. Then, we did the lunar hops. This mission to Mars is a major stepping stone to what she wants to do next, asteroid mining. She says we'll make amazing amounts of money."

I nodded. "It's pretty lucrative. I wouldn't mind tugging some mining equipment out to the belt."

She frowned. "You're like Claire, not afraid of anything, always willing to push farther out. Aren't you ever satisfied that you've gone far enough?"

I paused before responding, but I knew the answer right away. As soon as this mission ended, I'd be looking for another one and hoping it would be even more challenging. I shrugged. "I guess not."

Lena nodded. "Humankind needs people like you and Claire. You're the ones who push us forward." She wiped away a tear. "But I'm not like you and Claire. I need to see home."

§

In the middle of the twenty-second day of our voyage, I killed the engine and flipped *Asimov's Dream* around. We all got to float around for a few minutes.

I pointed Earth out to Lena, but we were so far away it just looked like a bright star in the sky. It didn't seem to bring her any comfort.

I re-engaged the thrusters. What had been our ceilings became our floors. We decelerated toward our rendezvous with Bennett Station, unsure of what awaited us there.

§

Bennett Station hung before us like a glimmering jewel. As the red landscape of Mars swept beneath us, I maneuvered *Asimov's Dream* in a slow sweep around the station.

Bennett Station consisted of three sections. The center section was the habitat module and the least interesting visually. It looked like a floating volleyball with windows and docking ports cut into it. Normally, the station operated without any human crew. The habitat module could host repair crews, such as ourselves, and provided radiation shielding for the station's computers.

The teleporter was a black plate one hundred meters in diameter suspended from a circular hoop by dozens of giant electric coils. Tendrils of blue energy periodically washed over the plate like snakes slithering across hot asphalt.

The last section was a global lattice of spinning metal one-hundred-fifty meters in circumference. Through the moving struts could be seen a miniature orange sun. Its flames churned furiously, occasionally leaping out and striking the cage that bound it. The windows of *Asimov's Dream* darkened to protect our eyes from the brilliant light generated by the reactor.

The teleporter required massive amounts of power that only a fusion reactor could provide, but the radiance produced by Bennett Station was one of the primary reasons it was built in orbit around

Mars instead of Earth. The artificial sunshine it created was intense enough to throw off the natural rhythms of a multitude of species on Earth. It probably would have been a welcome source of light for the Mars colony had the colony not perished decades before.

For the first few minutes of our arrival, we all just stared at the station in silence. We'd all seen it in pictures, but to see it in person was another thing entirely. Lena was the first to break the silence.

"So that's what a Planck fusion reactor looks like close up?"

I nodded.

Lena rubbed the side of her face. "It looks like a fire demon trying to escape from a zoo. How safe is that thing?"

"Very," said Claire. "Although there's nowhere near enough mass in the reaction to hold itself together, the metal structure rotating around it is comprised of super-cooled magnets which exert massive amounts of pressure. They both contain the reaction and increase the pressure to create the high temperatures needed to produce an energy generating reaction. The magnets are actually powered by the reaction itself, so there's no risk of them going offline while the reaction is still occurring."

I shook my head. "Claire smart. Me fly ship."

Claire rolled her eyes at me. Rex glared at me.

"Give us a complete sweep around the station," said Rex

I was already doing that, but I gave him a "Yes, sir," just to make him happy.

We swept around in front of the teleporter. I kept our ship at a safe distance.

"Can you imagine what it must be like to go through that thing?" asked Lena.

"Nope," I said.

"Why not? It seems exactly like the sort of thing you or Claire might do. Head out as far as humans have ever gone."

"But the teleporter doesn't take you anywhere. It disassembles you. Kills you on the spot. A copy of you gets created in the Alpha Centauri system, but the actual you doesn't get to go anywhere except oblivion."

Lena gasped in horror and looked at Claire. "Is that true?"

Claire nodded.

"But what about all those colonists who went through?" asked Lena.

"They sacrificed themselves to create enough human copies to get the colony going," I said. "Its population is increasing the old-fashion way now."

"They don't mention that in history class," said Lena.

I shrugged. "Yeah, they gloss over the suicide bit. But that's why people don't use the teleporter anymore. It's strictly for freight now."

"Enough chatter," said Rex. "Ryan, move us closer to the habitat module. There's something odd about that shadow there."

I complied, but waited till we were no longer in line with the teleporter. No disassembly for me, thanks. I tapped the maneuver thrusters lightly, and we slid forward. The shadow Rex saw came into focus, only it wasn't a shadow, it was a hole.

A two-meter hole had been ripped into the side of the habitat module. Jagged shards of metal pressed into the station meaning that whatever had done the damage had come from outside.

"Looks like a meteoroid strike," said Rex.

I didn't think so. If a meteoroid big enough to make a hole that size had hit the station, it would have turned the station into a shiny string of debris orbiting Mars. The kinetic energy of such an impact would have been catastrophic. But I didn't have any plausible alternatives to offer, so I kept quiet.

"Claire, any luck in raising the station bot?" asked Rex.

Claire shook her head. "I've been broadcasting hails since we arrived. No response."

I pointed at a cluster of antennas on the station. "Looks like the communication array is intact. Whatever the problem is, it's not the outside hardware."

Rex nodded. "Dock us, Ryan. We'll have to go in and see what the damage is. Claire, Lena, and I will suit up."

"Maybe I should head in instead of Lena. If we run into any difficulties, it would be good to have a medic and a pilot safe back here on the ship."

For once, God bless him, Rex agreed with me. "Good point. Lena, bring us in. Ryan, you're with me and Claire."

Claire gave Lena a peck on her cheek as Lena slid into the right-side pilot seat, and then Claire followed Rex out of the flight deck.

As I unstrapped myself from the left side pilot seat, Lena leaned over and whispered in my ear. "I'm going to strangle you in your sleep."

"What? You want to go into the spooky station?"

"I want to do my job, and I want to be with Claire."

"And I want a trained medic and pilot waiting for me back here in case my arm gets ripped off by some errant space debris. You'll be able to stop the bleeding and then fly me home. No one else could do that."

Lena glared at me.

"Oh come on, you get to dock," I pleaded. "Docking's fun."

Lena sighed and patted my arm. "Make sure you come back with Claire and both your arms."

§

As we moved through Bennett's narrow airlock, I was glad we were equipped with the latest skin-tight pressure suits. The old balloon models were not known for their mobility, and since we knew the structural integrity of the station had been compromised, we'd have to wear suits until we could patch the station up. Bennett didn't use rotation to simulate gravity, so we used magnetic boots to help us move around.

Bennett Station's airlock hatch had been left open. That was against every procedure. It wasn't the kind of mistake the last departing crew would have made. Rex must have been thinking the same thing because he remarked, "Maybe there was a fire, and the station bot decided it needed to depressurize the whole station to put it out."

It was pitch black inside. We turned on our helmet lamps. Claire found a control panel and activated the station's interior lighting. Only a few lights flickered to life. Large areas were left in shadow.

"The meteoroid strike must have cut some of the wiring," said Rex. His voice sounded scratchy over the radio.

I still wasn't buying the idea that a meteoroid had hit the station and somehow left it intact, but still had no alternative theory to offer.

I bumped into a large floating plastic bag of some kind. It was made of a shiny material I wasn't familiar with. The bag appeared to be filled with metal parts. I grabbed hold of it. An ingenious clasping mechanism held the bag shut. I opened the bag up and looked inside.

I'd found the station bot. It had been completely disassembled. I pulled out the bot's faceplate and showed it to Rex and Claire. "I don't think the bot is the one who left the airlock hatch open."

I had a theory now, and I hated it.

"Do you think the hatch was blown open by an explosion?" asked Rex. "I didn't see any damage on it."

"I think you're missing the big picture here," I said. "I also don't think the bot took itself apart and sealed itself inside of this odd storage bag."

Claire understood the implication right away. She opened her tool kit up and pulled out a large wrench. Rex took a moment longer to get my meaning.

"Think about it," I continued. "This bot was the only mobile piece of hardware on the station."

"So we have an intruder," said Rex. He began looking around the compartment we were in, his head lamp stabbing into every dark corner.

I'm sure he and Claire were both thinking the intruder was human. Even this was a leap in logic. There was a long history of cooperation among astronauts, no matter what nation or corporation they worked for. Space was just too dangerous to work in without a high level of trust. No matter how heated a rivalry might be back home, it got left behind when you left Earth. The idea that a fellow astronaut would break into Bennett Station and start sabotaging equipment was almost unfathomable.

"If that's the case," said Claire, "it's likely he or she isn't here anymore. There weren't any ships docked to the station."

"It's possible the intruders left someone behind," said Rex.

"Then why not re-pressurize the station?" asked Claire. "An intruder couldn't stay here long in just a pressure suit."

"Think about it," I said, "the hole in the side of the station…near the teleporter. Something came through."

"Are you suggesting the intruder is one of the colonists?" asked Rex.

I shook my head. "No, I'm suggesting something else came through, tore a hole in the station, opened all the hatches, and disassembled our bot."

"That's insane," said Rex.

I nodded because it was insane. The only aliens we humans had encountered so far were some plants, bacteria, and fungus on

Eden.

I moved farther into the compartment. A lot of computer hardware was missing. The atmospheric pressure controls were gone. Several more strange shiny bags floated near the walls.

"Something is taking this place apart for study," I said.

"We have to stop it," said Rex.

I looked at the tool in Claire's hand. "Our only weapon is a wrench."

As a kid I always assumed when I grew up and became an astronaut I'd get a ray gun of some kind. Well, here I was in space and no ray gun.

Rex held out his hands and said, "We can't just run home and tell Rosche we think there's an alien aboard their expensive space station. We have to confirm it. We have to see the damn thing."

I frowned. He was right. We had to be sure. And guess who got to lead the search? The engineer who was the only hope of repairing the station? The other engineer who was the only one who understood how the teleporter worked? Or the pilot, for whom there was a back-up? I might as well have stamped the word "expendable" on my forehead and changed into a red shirt.

I moved alongside the hatch that led to the teleporter controls and motioned Claire to come up alongside me. If there was a creepy-crawly in the next room, I wanted her to back me up.

"Lena says you're not afraid of anything, that true?" I asked her.

"I'm only afraid of one thing," she said.

"Is it aliens?"

She shook her head.

"Okay then, we should be good." I stepped through the hatch.

One of the interior lights in the room flickered on and off. The rest were dead. On the other side of the compartment was a meter-wide jagged hole through which I could see the sandy plains of

Mars. The notion that Mars was below me took hold of my brain. I had to pause for a moment and fight off a wave of vertigo. I managed to convince myself that Mars was up, that I was climbing toward it and not in any danger of falling through the hole.

I took a few more steps into the room. Darkness covered the corners. Computers lined the walls. My magnetic boots thumped on the floor. I reminded myself not to worry about the noise. There was no atmosphere in the station. I could only hear my boots because of the vibrations moving through my suit.

Something about the computers looked off. I shined my headlamp on the nearest one. What should have been a rectangular-shaped machine had an irregular, uneven form. The computer had been taken apart and put back together with new parts. A grainy, rust-covered material bulged out from the side of the machine.

I moved down the line of computers. All of them had been modified.

Claire stepped into the compartment. "See anything?"

"The computers have been upgraded."

"What?"

"I know, I can't even get a service tech to come out to my apartment on Earth. If we make contact with these guys, maybe we can talk them into providing us with IT support."

Claire moved past me and ran her gloved hand along the odd material on one of the machines. "What the hell is this?"

"No idea." My magnetic boots and I stomped over to one of the displays. Lines and lines of data scrolled down the screen. "What does this mean?"

Claire shrugged.

Rex entered the compartment and looked at the row of computers. "No. No. No. This is going to cost a fortune to repair!" He pushed me aside and looked at the monitor. "That's odd."

About a meter from the hole in the wall was a large window that offered a splendid view of the teleporter. Rex turned and looked out the window, so I did too. Waves of lightning with increasing frequency rolled across the massive dinner plate.

"What's odd?" I asked.

Rex looked back at the monitor. "Something's being copied. But the mass amount is more than the teleporter can handle."

A bolt of fear ran up my spine. "Is that your way of saying something big is coming through the teleporter?"

Rex nodded. "But it's too big. The computers can't process this amount of data."

"You mean the computers that have been modified with alien tech?"

"Good point." Rex typed a few commands into the console. "The buffer storage does appear to have been expanded exponentially."

I've never been one to panic. I've always been cool under pressure. It's a necessity for being a pilot. But the implications of what was happening filled me with terror.

"Shut it down!" I yelled.

"What? The teleporter? We can't," said Rex.

"Why not?"

"Safety protocol. Once something starts being copied, you can't stop the process. The original has already been destroyed. If we stopped the process, whatever is being copied would be lost forever."

"I'm okay with that," I said urgently.

"Well, the designers of the teleporter weren't. There's no way to stop the process once it's begun."

I took a few steps away from Rex and looked at the line of machines on the wall. "Which one of these things holds the data buffer?"

"All of them hold some part of it," answered Rex.

I kicked the nearest machine.

"What the hell are you doing?" screamed Rex.

"Trying to stop a Godzilla-sized alien from materializing on our doorstep!" I kicked the computer again. Its outer casing was amazingly robust. Who says you can't buy quality anymore? "Claire, can you smash this thing in with your wrench?"

Rex shoved me away from the computer. "We're supposed to be fixing the station, not trashing its equipment! Besides, what if it's the colonists that are coming through?"

"So, they snuck aboard the station and upgraded the computers with unknown technology to handle their secret, massive ship? Why no communications from them to tell us what they are up to? Rex, even if that thing coming through belongs to the colonists, something has gone terribly wrong with them. All I know is, I don't want whatever the hell is coming through in the same solar system as Earth!"

Claire stepped up behind me. "Ryan's right. We can't risk Earth."

Rex looked like he was about to offer a rebuttal, but when he opened his mouth no words came out. Instead, he opened his eyes as wide as they could go and looked behind me.

I spun around and saw a monster.

It dropped down from one of the dark corners and moved toward me. It had four spindly legs that gripped whatever surface they touched. Its body was an irregularly-shaped rectangle. Its oval head turned and looked at me with five sets of black lensed eyes. The creature appeared to be made from the same rust-colored material attached to the computers.

I raised my hands. "Hi there," I said slowly. "I hope you come in peace."

One of the monster's legs stabbed at my chest. Claire grabbed hold of the power pack on the back of my suit and pulled me out of the way as the monster's leg speared the space I had just occupied.

"Run!" shouted Claire. She pushed me toward the hatch we had first come through.

Rex stood his ground. "We can't just abandon the station to this thing!"

I jumped through the hatch, planted my feet on the floor of the next compartment, and twisted around to help pull Claire through.

Claire threw her wrench at the alien. It silently bounced off the monster. "We can't hurt that thing, commander. Let's go!"

Rex turned toward the hatch a moment too late. One of the monster's legs plunged into his torso. Anchoring itself on one leg, the alien brought its other two limbs up and rapidly disassembled Rex. His screams tore through my headphones and into my ears.

I tried to charge back in, but Claire held me back.

Something massive flashed into existence next to the station. I could only see part of its rust-colored hull through the hole and window.

Over the radio, Lena's voice tried to break through the screaming.

The alien continued to methodically take Rex apart. A shiny plastic bag emerged from the thing's body. Its nimble limbs carefully placed bits of Rex into the bag.

Claire pulled me away from the hatch and slammed it closed.

Rex went silent.

Claire sent out a broadcast. "Lena, prepare the ship for departure. Ryan, we have to use the time Rex gave us."

I nodded though I had no idea what she meant.

Lena's voice cut in. "Who was screaming? Guys, there's some sort of ship out here! It's huge!"

Claire pulled me farther into the habitat module. She touched her helmet against mine and said, "That thing tore its way into the station, so it won't take long for it to get through that hatch once it's done with poor Rex. You have to get back to the ship and get Lena and yourself clear of the station,"

"What about you? Where are you going?"

Claire walked away from me and slipped through the hatch to the fusion reactor controls module. "I have to stop them." She slammed the hatch shut.

I ran to the hatch. "Claire? Claire, what are you doing?" Through the hatch window I could see her taking apart a computer.

"I'm going to shut down the magnets that contain the fusion reaction." She said.

"That sounds like a bad thing, Claire."

"It is." She tossed a panel aside. "There are a lot of safety protocols I have to override to do it."

"So why are you doing it?"

"You know why. We have to destroy those things. It's likely the ship that just came through is full of aliens just like the one that tore apart Rex. We can't let them get to Earth. They'll dissect us all."

Lena pleaded over the radio, "Claire? Are you planning on blowing yourself up? You can't do that, Claire!"

Claire shook her head. "I'm sorry, baby."

I tried opening the hatch. Claire had locked it.

I tried to reason with her. "Hey, back on Earth we have lots of militaries with missiles and other weapons of destruction. Maybe we can blow 'em to hell before they ever land. You don't have to do this,"

"Can we take that chance?" asked Claire. "Can we risk all of humanity on that hope?" She pulled some wires out of the machine she was working on. "The colony on Eden had weapons too, just in case there was an encounter with aliens. We haven't heard from them in months. Odds are, they're gone."

I felt a vibration through the floor. I glanced back and saw spindly limbs pounding on the hatch behind me. The alien in the teleporter controls compartment had apparently finished bagging Rex and was trying to work its way to me.

"Can you set a timer?" I asked.

Claire shook her head. "No. No one ever planned on doing this. They designed the software to make sure the magnets never went offline while the fusion reactor was active. I'm trying to divert the power from them to another part of the station. The moment I succeed, the reaction will be released."

"Let me do it. No one will miss me. You have Lena."

Claire started typing on a keyboard. "You don't know how to do it. I'm not even sure I know how to do it. But I'm going to start giving it a try, so you need to get yourself and Lena away from the station."

I checked behind me again. An alien limb sawed through the wall next to the hatch. I watched for a moment as it cut through metal.

A soft whisper started echoing on the comms. It was Lena. "Please don't leave me, Claire. Please don't leave me."

I pounded on the hatch in front of me. "I can't let you do this, Claire!"

"It's not up to you." Claire looked at me through the hatch window. "I told you, I'm only afraid of one thing. I can't stand the thought of Lena being hurt. I need you to promise me you'll keep her safe."

Vibrations caused by the monster tearing its way into the habitat module caused the floor to tremble beneath my feet. I was out of time. I gritted my teeth and nodded at Claire.

I glanced behind me and sucked in a gulp of air. The thing was in the room with me. It surged forward, knocking aside the floating hatch door it had ripped from the wall. I jumped hard, tearing free of the grip my boots had on the floor. A rust-colored leg thrust beneath me and impacted the hatch I had just been looking through.

I pushed against the wall toward the airlock, flipping myself over as I flew through the habitat module. I grabbed onto the rim of the airlock and was about to pull myself through when something snagged my left boot.

One of the alien's legs had made contact with the bottom of my foot and stuck fast. I had a death grip on the airlock hatch and tried to pull myself into it with every ounce of my strength. I succeeded in causing the alien to shift toward me. It focused its five black eyes on me and anchored itself in the habitat module with its remaining three legs. It pulled back, and I felt my fingers slip. The monster that had me in its grip could tear through metal. I was no match for it in a tug of war.

The promise I'd made to Claire blared in my mind. I spoke into my helmet microphone as calmly as I could. "Lena, this thing's got me. Undock and do a full burn. Get clear of the station."

"Shut the hell up." Lena suddenly appeared in front of me and squeezed through the airlock hatch, clambering over me as if my body were a jungle gym. She uncapped a scalpel and sliced my boot open.

I pulled my foot free, and the monster yanked my boot away. A strange tingling sensation raced across my foot as my blood pushed up against the skin. The cuff of the pant leg tightened, sealing off the rest of my suit from the loss of pressure.

Holding onto Lena, I pulled us both into the station's airlock. Lena slammed the hatch shut and spun its locking mechanism. We bounded across the compartment and slid into *Asimov's Dream*. I turned the pressurization knob as soon as we closed the ship's hatch. For one, long, agonizing minute we held onto one another as the compartment filled with air, imagining at any moment the alien would break into the ship and tear us both apart.

The pressurization light flipped to green. I pulled my helmet off and welcomed stale, recycled air into my lungs. While Lena ditched her helmet, I pulled the door open to the main compartment of the ship. I dove through and, forgetting I had lost one of my boots, tried to run to the flight deck. The sock on my left foot turned out to be ineffective at adhering to the floor. I slipped, did an accidental somersault, and then tried to bunny hop to the pilot's seat.

Lena, using my shoulders as leverage, flew passed me. "Lose your other boot."

I hastily undid the straps, removed my remaining boot, and then kicked off the nearest wall. I flew into the flight deck and came to a stop by smashing my body into the back of the left-side pilot chair.

Lena was already strapping herself into the right-side chair. "Full burn?" she asked.

"Yeah," I said as I buckled myself in. "It's going to hurt, but we don't know how much time Claire can give us."

Lena nodded and flipped a pair of safety switches. A tear broke free of her face and hung in the air.

I glanced at her and said, "I know you went back for her, but thanks for stopping and saving me."

Lena shook her head slightly. "I wanted to save you too. I wanted to save anyone I could." She toggled a switch on the control panel arming the rocket. "Let's get out of here while we still can."

I nodded and disengaged the ship from the docking port of Bennett station. As we drifted away from the station, I set the main engine throttle to maximum.

This was going to suck.

"One minute full burn. Sit up straight. Head back against the seat," I said. "Engaging main engine in three, two, one…"

I ignited the engine. An invisible anvil of force slammed down on my chest, crushing me into my chair. Our bodies went from experiencing no gravity to weighing ten times what they would on Earth. The edge of my vision went black. I felt as if I were hurtling down a tunnel.

Out of the corner of my eye, I saw something bright appear on the rearview display. Unable to move my head, I moved my eyes down and to the side and focused on the monitor. I watched as bursts of light marked the death of the magnets containing Bennett Station's fusion reactor. The reaction burst free, consuming its lattice cage in a rapidly growing ball of fire.

I only saw the alien spacecraft for a moment. Dreadfully long, it resembled a rust-colored cigar. It hung menacingly near the teleporter plate that had assembled it, ready to visit Earth.

The growing reaction reached it. The miniature sun blackened its hull and then tore it apart.

Bennett Station vanished into a whirling firestorm. The reaction continued to grow, burning bright against the reddish-brown backdrop of Mars. For a moment, I worried it might consume the planet, but when the fireball had grown ten times its original size, it fell apart.

Huge chunks of plasma tore away from the reaction. Pieces of burning mass blew out in every direction. An explosion tore the heart out of the artificial sun. I gasped as debris from the station and alien ship hurled toward us at impossible speed.

Deciding I didn't want to see my death coming, I looked away from the display. Protocol dictated I yell "Brace!" when a collision was imminent, but it seemed pointless since Lena and I were pinned to our chairs.

I closed my eyes as wreckage tore through our ship. Alarms

blared as compartments lost pressurization. We shouldn't have taken our helmets off. A pair of emergency spares were stored just below the control console, but they might as well have been back in the airlock. We were experiencing so many G's I could barely flex my fingers.

Automated hatches slid shut, sealing off parts of the ship that had lost atmosphere. *Asimov's Dream* shuddered, but we remained on course. The engine shut down and my body decompressed. I could move again. I could breathe again.

§

The crew compartment Claire and Lena had been using suffered a direct hit, and the ventral airlock was shorn clean off the ship. We still have the topside airlock and the crew compartment Rex and I had been using, so we'll be fine. The engine, miraculously, appears to have been undamaged.

Due to our minute of full thrust, I could only set our acceleration toward home at around zero point-nine G's, but that's still fairly comfortable.

My foot's brief exposure to vacuum left it an odd purple color, but Lena said it will return to normal. She appears to have gotten through our adventure without any injury…well any physical injury.

We've both cried over the loss of Claire. I wish I'd known her better. I've even shed a few tears for Rex. We didn't get along, but he did his job the best way he knew how. He didn't deserve what happened to him.

We've been in contact with Rosche Corporation. They're having trouble accepting that their station is gone, and that it's gone because of alien contact. That fact will weigh heavily on all of humanity in the coming years.

The aliens made use of our teleporter, so that means they don't have some magical rocket capable of traveling faster than the speed of light. However, they came from the nearest star system so, depending on their level of technology, they could reach Earth in as few as eight years or as long as a century. I hope it's closer to the latter, because we'll need all the time we can get to prepare for their arrival.

Michael D. Burnside is a graduate of Ohio University. By day, he earns a living as a systems analyst. His interests include gaming, science, computer technology, history, politics, and, of course, writing. His fiction writing includes steampunk, science fiction, fantasy, and horror. His stories have been featured in multiple anthologies, including *Fossil Lake: An Anthology of the Aberrant*, *Fossil Lake II: The Refossiling*, *Beautiful Lies, Painful Truths Vol. II*, and *Ink Stains Vol. 8*. His short stories have also been featured in magazines such as *Devolution Z*, *Outposts of Beyond*, and *Gathering Storm Magazine*. One of his latest stories, "The Devil of Greystern Castle," appears in the Spring 2023 edition of *Dragon Gems*. Michael lives in Dayton, Ohio, with his wife, two giant dogs, and lots of cats. Read more nice things about him, as well as some free stories, at www.michaelburnside.com.

The Wawa Stick

By Karl El-Koura

"If you're attacked by a yancee, set your wawa stick to its highest setting and fire, fire, fire! Attacked by a yancee and don't have a wawa stick? Enjoy being yancee-food. That's what you get for ignoring or failing to remember the first rule of exploring Banou— always carry a fully-charged wawa stick."

—from *A Guide to the Safe Exploration of the Planet Banou*, by E.L. Mysher

§

JAN DIDN'T HAVE A WAWA STICK. When her husband's goon dumped her on this miserable planet, he didn't bother providing one.

"Enjoy being yancee-food," he said as he pushed her out the back of the hover-truck. "Enjoy being yancee-food, you stupid" and then some choice words.

Jan was smart enough not to wait on the ground, at least. Despite Ms. Mysher's pessimism, Jan was certain she could avoid the yancees by climbing one of the very tall trees in the small forest nearby.

Jan was wrong; halfway up she saw a yancee waiting for her on one of the thick branches extending from the top of the tree. She broke off a branch the size of her arm and approached. The yancee stared at her.

"A branch?" he said. At ten feet, the yancee stood twice her height; nevertheless, that was short for a yancee. Jan realized that

172

this was probably a child. "You're going to attack me with a branch?"

"This isn't a branch," Jan said; it was the first time since university that she'd spoken Yantook, but she managed to get the words out. "It's a wawa stick."

The yancee made a low-pitched rumbling sound, his species' equivalent to a laugh. "I just saw you break it off the tree!"

"This? I've been carrying this with me all along."

"It doesn't even look like a wawa stick." But the yancee wasn't moving any closer, and he wasn't laughing anymore.

"Doesn't it? Whatever it looks like, I think you'll find that it feels like a wawa stick." She pointed the branch at him.

"Don't!" the yancee screamed, but didn't bother waiting to see if she'd comply. He dove through the leaves, as if into a swimming pool, and caught hold of a lower branch. Swinging from branch to branch, he made his way to the ground. Without looking back, he fled, arms swaying in panic above his head.

Jan sat on the thick branch at the top of the tree, her feet dangling below her. The large red sun was setting, the small yellow one was rising; she stared at the different colors as they swirled in the sky. She tried to think of how she could get off Banou, back to Earth, back into her husband's presence, and accomplish then what she should've done the last time she saw him: end the miserable bastard's miserable existence.

But her mind kept wandering, returning to the past, back to the point, almost a year ago now, when things had gone from bad to worse...

§

"Why do men cheat? Because they're men, that's why. The best way to deal with infidelity is to forgive and forget and try harder to keep your man sexually and emotionally satisfied in the future."

—from *Why Men Cheat (And What You Can Do About It)*, by Joseph Rodnesky, Ph.D

§

Getting into her husband's office was easy.

"Hi Ernie," Jan said to the night guard, pretending not to notice the way his eyes lit up when he saw her. "I'm here to surprise my husband. Is that okay?"

"Anything for you," he said, sliding his hand over his terminal's keyboard to silence the alarms. "Will you come back before you leave? I want to show you something. You'll like it, I promise."

"Of course," she said, but in a purely friendly tone. Even now, she still felt like a married woman and didn't want to lead the young man on (the *handsome* young man, she had to admit).

On the top floor of the building, Peter's secretary wasn't at her desk. Not that Jan had expected her to be. The geniuses hadn't even bothered to lock the door. Peter and his secretary were on the black leather couch at the side of his office.

"Well, well," Jan said.

The bouncing blonde turned her head, and then fell to the ground as Peter pushed her off of him.

"This isn't what you think."

Jan pulled out a police-grade camera from her coat's pocket and snapped verifiably authentic pictures. Peter sitting on the couch cupping his groin (as if there was that much to hide, Jan thought), check. Naked blonde secretary scrambling for her clothes, check.

"Dumb man," Jan said. "Don't you know the prenup is void if you cheat?" Despite Dr. Rodnesky's advice, after suspecting her husband of having a wandering penis, Jan decided to stick around only long enough to gather evidence that would stand up in court.

"You're divorcing me?" Even as his mistress struggled to put on her skimpy black lace underwear, Peter managed to sound hurt.

"Silly man," Jan said. "What else does one do with a husband who can't keep his pants on?"

Peter's secretary was babbling apologies; Jan told her to shut up. The secretary gathered the clothing she hadn't yet managed to put on and slipped out the door, all while babbling more barely coherent apologies.

Peter hadn't moved. He sat on the black leather couch, shielding his groin with his hands. "You're not divorcing me."

Jan repeated his words. *"You're not divorcing me."* It was childish, but being mocked was Peter's number-one pet peeve.

"That's funny, Jan. But I'm quite serious."

His gaze drifted past her. Jan turned around.

In the doorway stood his beautiful blonde secretary, clothed and pointing a gun at Jan's head.

When Jan returned her attention to Peter, he'd slipped on his pants. "As clever as she is beautiful, don't you think? And she always knows just what to do to help me out of a tight spot."

Jan cursed herself inwardly for letting the little princess leave the room, but tried not to show her frustration. "You're going to kill me?"

"Silly girl," Peter said. "What else does one do with a gold-digging wife who threatens to take away one's fortune and ruin one's reputation? But don't worry, my love—Holly and I wouldn't dream of killing you ourselves."

He walked over to his mahogany desk and retrieved a small book from one of its drawers. "Banou is one of the most dangerous planets in the universe," he said, tossing the book at Jan. She didn't try to catch it. "Pick that up. It's a long trip to Banou. Spend some of the time reading up on all the ways you can die there. Consider it a little going-away present."

§

"There are no miracles."

—from *A Scientific Treatise Refuting the Ontological Possibility of Miracles,* by Dr. A. R. Bryce

§

Jan spent hours at the top branch of the tree. She ate sandwiches made of red berries wrapped in purple, star-shaped leaves. Neither was poisonous, according to the book her husband had given her and which she'd read a thousand times on the eleven-month journey to Banou.

At times she almost wished the book was wrong. But she felt fine, after crunching through the rough leaves and forcing herself to swallow the slightly bitter berries. Physically she felt fine. But how long could she possibly sur—

In the next instant she found herself scrambling down the tree. She ignored the pain as the jagged branches cut her. More than once her foot missed a branch, and she caught herself just before shifting her weight. Finally, her right foot found the ground.

She looked east beyond the small forest, where from the tree-top she'd seen the advancing group of yancees, their lanky bodies almost a blur in the distance. They were closer now, maybe a hundred of them, the whole tribe come to hunt her in case she did have a wawa stick. She could almost hear their shrieking. Their long, gangly, monkey-arms held weapons—clubs and rocks and what looked like axes and anything else they could use to bash in her head and chop her up.

She ran, by the same instinct that sent her down the tree like a toddler climbing down stairs when she's being play-chased. And she was giggling too, just like the toddler might, just as if the yancees wanted to play, just as if they weren't hunting her down to make dinner out of her.

She was giggling at the absurdity of her situation. Her short legs were no match for their long ones; they'd be on top of her in no time. She was already out of the forest, if the small group of tall trees could be called a forest. She was headed straight for the cliff near where her husband's goon had dumped her, perhaps out of a twisted brand of mercy, perhaps on her husband's instruction.

And now? Would she jump off rather than be torn apart by a pack of screaming yancees?

She reached the edge of the cliff, no longer laughing, just panting for breath. One miracle in a lifetime, was that too much to ask? She could take a few steps back, run, jump…and fly, her one miracle-wish granted; and soar to safety, halfway around the planet or all the way off the planet if need be.

She turned around, looked at the approaching gaggle of yancees. They weren't far from her now. She wouldn't jump, she knew. She'd fight. She'd die, of course, and probably die horribly. Maybe they'd push her off by accident and end her misery early, but she'd fight for as long as she could before they tore her limb from limb. Tears streamed down her face, blurring her vision.

She heard and felt something from behind her, like a great bird swooping into the canyon. She looked over her shoulder, but nothing was there. Had she imagined the gust of wind?

As she stood staring, something floated out of the mouth of the canyon. A great bird made of metal. A small spaceship. And through the window, she saw something she never thought she'd see again. A human face.

As she continued staring, trying to see despite her tear-blurred vision, trying to confirm that this wasn't a hysterical hallucination, she thought she saw the figure raise a hand and wave at her….

§

Two hours later, Jan sat in a plush purple bathrobe, drinking tea. She'd spent an entire hour in the shower, which was as much hot water as the small spaceship could pump out, or she would've stayed longer. She smelled nice; she had missed smelling nice.

"I didn't recognize you," she said.

Ernie smiled, then stroked his beard. "You like it?"

She shook her head.

He laughed. "I'll shave it off, then."

"Okay, I'm ready," she said, putting down her cup on the table. Her tongue passed over her teeth; she'd almost used up all the toothpaste, too. She was good to kiss now. She pushed the thought out of her mind.

Ernie shrugged. "There isn't much to tell. I wanted to show you a drawing I was working on and you promised to come back, but you never did. I went up to Mr. Dortowski's office, but he was gone; his helicopter was gone too. The next day Mr. Dortowski said you'd disappeared, he didn't know where. He said you'd been talking about getting away from everything and everyone and starting your life over. I didn't believe a word of it."

"Thank you."

Ernie smiled, his eyes twinkling. He stroked his beard again. "I went to the cops and told them what I knew, but it wasn't enough. They couldn't move on Mr. Dortowski without evidence. Believe me, they'd love nothing more—they'd nail the bastard to the wall if they could." He looked up at her suddenly. "Sorry." Before Jan could say anything, he went on, "I was fired by then, of course. So I really had nothing better to do than to come after you myself."

Instead of returning his playful smile, Jan stuck out her tongue at him. He laughed, then looked back down at the space on the table in front of him. *Such a nervous boy*, Jan thought.

"How did you know they took me off-world?"

Ernie looked back up at her. "Tip from the cops. They said one of Mr. Dortowski's ships blasted off the night you disappeared. Nothing illegal about that, but the detective thought I might want to know."

Ernie gave her another of his smiles—she could get used to looking at those smiles, especially the dimples that dotted each end like punctuation. He stood, picked up her empty cup, and walked to the sink.

"Ernie? I think you're forgetting something."

When he turned, she looked around the room, her gaze tracing out the curve of the spaceship's hull.

"Oh," he said, turning his back to her again. "I borrowed this." His voice was low, even a little sulky.

"You mean stole, right? This is one of my husband's ships?"

He nodded. "I'm sorry, but I didn't have—" He paused as she wrapped her arms around him.

"You've got a strange sense of morality, Ernie. You saved my life. I'm not going to judge you for stealing one of Peter's ships to do it."

"My security codes still worked." Ernie's breathing was quick; she could feel his heartbeat race. "I just walked right in and took it." He gulped, loudly.

"Does this spaceship have a bedroom?" she said, turning him around.

He stared into her eyes, then nodded.

"Will you show me?"

Again he nodded.

"Sometime soon?"

"Ye-es." He cleared his throat. "I mean, yes, of course I'll show you. I very much want to show you. I—"

"You're babbling, Ernie."

"I know, I do that." He took a deep breath and let it out slowly. "Just give me our destination and I'll set the course. Anywhere you want."

She took a step back. "What do you mean? Earth, of course."

His face dropped. "We can't go there." He reached out for her, held her by the upper arms. "I thought we could go somewhere together, somewhere far away from your husband's reach, sell this spaceship and buy a house, start a new life together. We can go anywhere."

"I want to go to Earth."

"Why?" His hands dropped away from her. "You want to confront your husband? He'll kill us both."

"He sent me to that planet to die, Ernie. He can't...I just couldn't be at peace if he got away with that." Ernie looked away. "I have a plan."

"It's too dangerous. Best case, he has me thrown in jail."

"You have to trust me. I have a—where are you going?"

"To set course for Earth," he said, stopping. "If you'll follow me, I'll show you to your room." He continued walking, without waiting to see if she'd follow.

§

"A spectral glow of prismatic and iridescent reds and greens and blues floated around him like light from a million microscopic vibrating diamonds. I'm not lying. I'm not crazy."

—from *I Saw A Ghost*, by Justine Tan

§

Jan walked into her husband's office at the top of his forty-story high building. She wore clothes as similar to the last time he saw her as she could find—black slacks and a long-sleeved sky-blue turtleneck. But this time she walked into the office from outside, and walked through his wet bar and through the all-glass coffee table before coming to a stop in front of his desk. She didn't say anything, but he looked up. His face fell, his jaw dropping open. He stared at her. He drew in breath. His lips trembled, looked like he was about to cry. Instead, his lips pursed together and his whole body began to shake.

The look on Jan's face sustained his laughter, and he glanced up at her from time to time as if to refresh himself. *"This* is what you were up to?" he said, and then laughed some more.

Finally Peter stood and walked around the desk. He waved his hands through her neck, as if beheading her with karate chops.

"Not bad, not bad." He punched her in the stomach, his arm going right through. He began to shadow box with her. "Not bad execution, I'll give you that. But the idea—do you really take me for such an idiot?"

He began to dry-hump her hologram, but she stepped away. He laughed. "So this was your big idea. What did you think, I'd go running to the cops?" He put his hands together at the wrist and held them up. "You must arrest me! I've done horrible things, I killed my wife and now her ghost is haunting me. I can still hear the beating of her heart!" He dropped his hands. "Oh Jan, give me some credit." He shook his head. "Too much reading has made you stupid."

The look of disappointment, failure, and anger on her face made Peter howl with laughter.

She waited for him to finish. "You're pretty smug for a guy who failed to do something as simple as killing his own wife."

"Me, smug?" He shrugged. "I failed once, but I won't fail again." He stepped up to her and looked into her eyes. "It's funny, because I really am talking to a dead woman."

Jan ignored the threat. "You found the transmitter?"

"No-*o-o-o*, Jan. Your boyfriend's cleverly disguised identity fooled me. And I didn't notice that we had a new janitor working for us and that this new janitor planted a hologram transmitter in my office. You're just that clever and I'm just that stupid."

"How come you didn't disable it, then?"

"Curiosity," he said. "And to toy with you, to give you a few moments of thinking you were oh-so-smart before I showed you how dumb you really are. And, I must admit, another reason. As soon as you projected yourself into my office, Mr. Hendley—you must remember him from your long trip to Banou?—began tracking your signal. He should be knocking on your door…oh, momentarily, I'd say." He walked over to his desk; he sat in the chair and brought up a screen. "I'm going to watch you die, honey; I want to make sure it's done right this time."

Jan stared at him for a long time. "Silly man," she said, finally.

"What?" Peter's gaze jumped from the screen to her. "What's going on?"

"You didn't disable the hologram transmitter. But didn't you realize that the transmitter is also a receiver—and a recorder?"

He stood, pushing himself away from the desk.

"Mr. Hendley is under arrest, I'm afraid." She looked away from the screen to watch the cops rifle through his pockets. With a lift of her eyebrows, she turned back to the camera and the picture of Peter on the screen. "Wow, honey, all those sharp doohickeys just to kill little old me?"

Peter started cursing.

Jan gave him a stern look. "Police officers are coming to see you now. Have some self-respect. Don't be a gibbering fool, okay?"

"I'll kill you for this," he said, his body shaking. "I'll kill you and your boyfriend and everyone who ever said a single nice word to you. I swear it!"

"I'm sorry, honey," she said, looking down at him. "But we just had to help the cops. They were so nice to Ernie when he brought back the spaceship and said how sorry he was he stole it. We just had to do something nice for them in return."

From his desk drawer, Peter pulled out a small silver object.

For the first time, real concern filled Jan's heart. "Don't do something stup—"

"Shut up!" Gun trained on the door, he stood against the windows at the other end of the office. "Tell them not to come in here. Tell them if they try to break down the door I'll kill them all."

"Tell them not to go in!" Jan said, turning to Ernie, the cops, the technicians working the equipment. "Let me talk to him fir—"

The loud whine of laser shots snapped her attention back to the screen.

"Oh, thank God," she said.

Her husband held his right hand—it looked like a lumpy mass of pink flesh now—cradled in his left hand, but otherwise seemed unharmed.

Peter thrashed against the officer holding him. "Tell her to shut up! I never want to hear her voice again." He began to weep. "Just tell her to shut up, okay?"

§

Jan and Ernie sat across from each other at a table on the beach. This week their honeymoon took them to a quiet resort in the south of Mexico, and this restaurant had quickly become their favorite place from which to watch the setting sun.

A waiter walked across the sand to clear away their empty plates.

"Another bottle, please," Ernie said, and the waiter nodded as he loaded his tray.

Jan leaned back in her chair and sipped her wine. "What was I saying?" It was a beautiful night, almost cloudless. They'd spent the day swimming and lying on the beach, and she felt both fully rested and completely exhausted.

"You were saying that your ex-husband is dumber than a yancee."

Jan nodded. "Right. Yes. I was able to convince a yancee that something that wasn't a weapon was one. But I was able to convince Peter that something that was a weapon wasn't."

"At least the yancee erred on the side of caution," Ernie said.

"And my husband fell for the oldest trick in the book and confessed his sins to a running recorder, because he thought I was just like him and wanted to play mind games forever."

The waiter returned with another bottle and refilled their glasses.

"Please remind me never to cross you, Jan."

She laughed, and then pointed at his chin.

Ernie stroked his beard. "This again? OK, you don't like it, it's gone."

Jan laughed again because he'd been saying that for the last year. "Actually," she said, "I think it's finally starting to grow on me."

"Oh, good!" Ernie's blue eyes twinkled in the fading light. "Because really I have zero intention of shaving it off."

She play-kicked him under the table, then let her bare foot slide up his leg.

"Check, please," Ernie said in a faint voice, to no one.

Jan giggled and dropped her foot.

The horizon glowed a rich orange. She leaned across the table and placed her hands in Ernie's. Together, in silence, they watched the last few rays of the sun sink below the horizon.

Karl El-Koura lives with his family in Canada's capital city and works a regular job by day while writing fiction at night. Visit www.ootersplace.com to learn more about his work.

Wait, before you leave...

The goal of *Stupefying Stories* is pretty simple: to bring you a strong mix of terrific stories, written by talented authors whose work you may not have read before, and to deliver a lot of good new reading at an affordable price. This is what we've been doing for the past twelve-plus years. This is what we want to keep doing, but to do so, we need your help. If you enjoyed this book, please:

Write a quick review of this issue, or at least rate it.

Follow us on Facebook @ facebook.com/Stupefying Stories

Follow us on Twitter @StupefyingSF

Check out our website @ stupefyingstories.blogspot.com

But most of all, **tell your friends about us!** Remember, likes and hearts are nice, but shares and retweets boost the signal!

Thank you,
Bruce Bethke
Editor, Publisher, and Executive Cat-Herder-in-Chief
Stupefying Stories | Rampant Loon Media LLC